CAROL MARGARET TETLOW

Change of Mind

First published by Editions Dedicaces LLC in 2017

Copyright © Carol Margaret Tetlow, 2017

First Edition

ISBN: 978-1-77076-644-0

This book was professionally typeset on Reedsy.
Find out more at reedsy.com

Contents

Chapter One

'What time did you say your appointment was with Dr Britton?' Joan's patience was wearing thin. This was the third time she had asked the question and she was still struggling to make herself heard.

She glared at the wrinkled elderly lady, half hidden by a dark green felt hat, who was only just tall enough to see over the counter.

'Eleven thirty, as it always is.'

Miss Chisholm was not one to be intimidated by the likes of a lowly receptionist. She glared back with equal ferocity, jutting out her chin. 'So tell him I'm here. He might be able to see me sooner.' She checked her scrawny, freckled wrist around which a watch dangled loosely like a bracelet and sucked her bottom lip noisily.

'But you're over half an hour early. It's a fine day, why don't you go off and walk round the market square for a little while and come back. You can see how busy the reception area is...'

Joan's protestations were useless as Miss Chisholm wafted an arm dismissively in her direction and shuffled over to a row of seats, where there was a solitary vacancy, dragging her tartan shopping trolley behind her.

'Let him know I'm here,' she repeated. 'Your colleague always does. That one over there with the black hair, which ought to be tied back. Not hygienic in a doctors' surgery, if you ask me. Think of the germs. I'll wait here outside his surgery and look at one of these old magazines. I've read them all before, you know, it's time you got some up to date ones. When he sees me he'll probably see me early.'

Yes, to get rid of you, thought Joan wearily noticing that there was still a good hour or more until her lunch break. The telephones had rung insistently and incessantly and there always seemed to be a queue of miserable-looking faces to be dealt with. What did patients expect these days? A decade ago, they'd have treated receptionists with respect but not now. Honestly, what they had to put up with, the rudeness, the demands, until the patients got want they wanted. They should try her job for a day and see how it felt.

Joan had started working at the surgery some nine years ago when her son Simeon was nicely settled at nursery and she was able to rely on her mother Ivy to pick him up and give him his tea. This excellent arrangement meant that she could work full time and thereby bring home an adequate if not enormous income, which, added to her mother's small private pension, was enough to support the three of them – just. Even so, luxuries were few and far between. Her mother loved spending time with her grandson, even if she did give him chocolate every day and those brightly coloured sweets that made him overactive and uncontrollable, just before bedtime. Initially it had seemed an ideal arrangement but Ivy's health was far less robust now than it had been.

Greg Bickerdike, Joan's erstwhile husband, had left longer ago than she cared to remember and good riddance. She chose to forget those hideous years and rather wished that she had forgotten his name as well. Theirs had never been a match made in heaven. She had little if anything good to say about him now and indeed never had. It still made her shudder with disgust when she remembered the moment when, after plying her with gin and lime, he had pinned her against that hard, cold wall in the dank ginnel between the pub and the fish and chip shop, fumbling to gain access to her unprepared and unwilling body, whispering endearments he did not mean. This violation was only trumped by the appalling revelation two months later that she was pregnant. To her amazement, when confronted with the grim reality of what had happened, he offered to marry her and the fear of being alone with a child had made her accept. She had hoped that he did want to make a go of it but her mother had simply muttered that people don't change and had refused to buy a new dress for the wedding at the local registry office.

Good does not necessarily come after bad, dreams do not always come true and his behaviour did not improve. He had never been in her eyes the least bit supportive, financially or emotionally and had left her to do all the work with the baby. A second child conceived after an equally unsatisfactory coupling shortly after the birth of the first was the final indignity. Who was it said that you couldn't get pregnant while breast feeding? Keeping the awful truth to herself, Joan had an abortion, unable to contemplate another dependent spawned by such an unfeeling human.

Greg was not one to embrace family life. Faced with the prospect of time at home where the cries and tantrums of his son shattered the peace and quiet, or rather blocked out the sound from his television sport, Greg spent increasing amounts of his day in the pub with his mates where, apparently, the enormous responsibilities of being in the darts team far outweighed those of being a father. It had been such a relief when he left. Simeon was just walking and Roger, as she had planned to call him – it would have been just her luck to have another dependent man in her life - would have been trying to sit up, if he had been given a chance at life.

Lucky for Simeon that he would have no memory of his father.

Rumours abounded that Greg had taken up with a part-time teaching assistant who, on Saturdays, worked in the local garden centre, an appropriate place for love to blossom. He moved ten miles away to Ripon but Joan didn't care. She ignored the annual Christmas card complete with ten-pound note that arrived for her attention at the surgery, stuffing the money immediately into the charity box on the front reception desk, feeling that at least it had gone to a good cause.

She had a brief dalliance with a butcher she met on an internet dating site, at the insistence of her mother, who kept telling her there were plenty more fish in the sea. Joan felt she was being eyed up as a potential carcase. Even the promise of free cuts of meat did not stop her being repulsed by the fact that his fingernails were always dirty and that he only had one shirt for going out in and that had brown sweat stains under the arms. What tiny spark might have burned between them soon petered out after their third date when his sole topic of conversation was the new apple, cinnamon and pork sausages he had created that day.

Hardly surprising then, that Joan's opinion of men was not particularly high. She had little patience for them when they came to the desk for their appointments and found it especially distasteful when they asked for a female doctor specifically. In Joan's eyes this was not appropriate and she would, more often than not, book them in with the male partners, either Dr Diamond or Dr Britton, and then assume a look of innocence when they turned up and pretend she had misunderstood.

She enjoyed her work overall and rightly took pride in her not inconsiderable skills. Over the years she had worked her way diligently, if somewhat slowly, to the role of senior receptionist. This gave her a certain sense of power, to say nothing of the rather smarter uniform and she enjoyed seeing the less forceful plead for some time with the doctor. Her fellow receptionists were a good team though they needed to have a careful watch over them and she had never understood to this day why on earth Elliott Douglas, the practice manager, had employed Gary, a slightly effete young man with gelled hair, despite her admonitions that a male receptionist would be trouble. To date, he had proved himself to be popular with the patients and other staff but Joan was watching him, waiting for him to slip up. It was only a matter of time.

The doctors at Teviotdale medical centre were pleasant enough. Dr Ed Diamond was always chatty but very young and sometimes did home visits on his bicycle and Dr Ellie Bonnington seemed to have it all, beauty, personality, intelligence. It was all right for some but didn't seem fair.

Without a doubt, Joan's favourite was John Britton. Always smiling and laughing. He even brought in cakes on quite a regular basis that his wife had baked. Not many doctors thought of their staff like that. Nothing ever seemed to get him down, unlike some of the others who looked as though they had the weight of the world on their shoulders – a good description of Clare Jennings and Faith Faber. They were both inevitably in the building before anyone else and last out in the evenings. Their surgeries always ran late and their patients were elderly, arduous with multifaceted pathology or young, feckless and unable to cope with what life dealt them. Joan had also noticed that they worked through their lunch more often than not, taking bites out of sandwiches with one hand while typing with the other, pausing only to blow crumbs off the keyboard or take a gulp of tea or coffee. Living like that wasn't doing either of them any good. They should be at home with their families more. Get their priorities right. She wasn't one hundred percent sure but Joan thought she might have smelled alcohol on Dr Jennings' breath the other day and she always seemed to be sucking sweets. Peppermints. That would need keeping an eye on too for it was a well-known fact how doctors were at risk of alcoholism.

Joan paused to massage her neck and temples. Her muscles were tense and stiff. Hardly surprising after the hassles of the morning which had started out badly with no breakfast because Simeon was playing up and then no mid-morning break because it was all too frantic. She had consulted Dr Britton a short while ago, complaining of headaches, but the current tablets weren't really helping at all. Supposed to prevent the headaches from even coming on in the first place, all they were managing to do was make her feel quite disorientated at times, as though her head wasn't quite attached to her body and it was imperative she had all her wits about her, not simply at work but with Simeon becoming increasingly difficult to look after too, to say nothing of Ivy's needs. She needed to have another chat with the doctor, preferably Dr Britton. After all, continuity of care was vital – all the partners and the practice manager were always emphasising this, so it was only correct that she went back to see him as he had prescribed last time.

Miss Chisholm was muttering to herself unintelligibly as she prised open the sticky pages of a glossy magazine, intermittently looking up expectantly as the next patient was called in. She carefully tore out a page and folded it up to take home. Shaking her head slowly, Joan turned to her computer and looked at the appointment situation. Dr Britton was fully booked all day. Dr Bonnington however had one free slot in ten minutes' time. There must have been a last-minute cancellation, Joan mused. Without a moment's hesitation, she swapped Miss Chisholm over to see Dr Bonnington and then booked herself into the now available appointment with Dr Britton. Smiling, both outwardly and inwardly, she stood up, smoothed down her hair, straightened the waistband of her skirt and happily went to the front desk. She leant over and shouted.

'Miss Chisholm? I'm afraid Dr Britton's been called out on an emergency but I've managed to fit you in with Dr Bonnington as a special favour, so if you'd like to go round the corner and wait outside her room, she'll see you in a moment or two.'

'But...'

'I'm so sorry. That's the best I can do for you today. Other patients might be upset, but I know you'll understand.' Joan interrupted with an air of finality and turned away.

As a disgruntled Miss Chisholm shuffled off, amidst more muttering, with her squeaky trolley, Joan watched until she was out of sight and then sat down in the newly vacated chair.

The door opened.

'Ah, Joan, come on in and have a seat. I hadn't spotted you in my surgery list...'

Joan beamed, stood up and followed Dr Britton into his surgery, willingly.

Chapter Two

John Britton sat back in his chair and surveyed Joan with a broad smile, before rotating to his computer to bring up her records. His surgery was a cornucopia of photographs and personal memorabilia, which he insisted on keeping despite noises from on high that dust and bacteria would be attracted. He loved to be reminded constantly of his family and home, which meant so much to him – his theory being that it made him a better doctor for feeling comfortable and secure. A marriage that had lasted over forty years was something to cherish and celebrate, along with four grown-up children, eight grandchildren, to say nothing of the collection of dogs and cats that had been part of the family along the way.

Among the personal items were posters promoting good health. How to eat well, be checked for Chlamydia, stop smoking, find a counsellor and avoid diabetes. If he were honest, he'd have taken those down, as it was his belief that patients came to discuss their problems with him and not take in their surroundings.

His was a room that the cleaners fought over – to avoid. None of them relished the tidying and dusting, having to move all those objects, put straight the photos and leave everything as they'd found it. They had moaned to Elliot, who had in turn passed the message on to John, who had smiled and done...nothing. In the end, they'd come up with a rota, so that each one of them had a turn, however reluctantly. It took as long to do his room as it did all the other consulting rooms put together.

That day he was wearing his usual selection of comfy clothes. Cord trousers in lovat green, a tweed jacket with leather elbow patches, a checked shirt, which narrowly avoided matching the jacket and a red bow tie. Despite gentle persuasion from Faye, his wife, he refused to be parted from his bow tie, which he felt was a mark of slight eccentricity that his patients admired.

Turning back to Joan, he leant forward slightly as a sign for her proceed. She needed little encouragement and was soon prattling on about her headaches – which part of her head they were in, what made them worse, what – if anything – eased them and what she had tried to make them better. She knew in advance what questions he was going to ask and thought she was doing him a kindness by saving him the bother.

She liked his room, his roll-top desk, the jumbled decor. She liked his slightly crumpled appearance as well. None of the others held the same appeal. Dr Diamond's surgery was on the verge of being stark with only a couple of framed photos he had taken from the top of some cliff he'd been climbing to brighten it up. Dr Bonnington's was more like a child's playroom and on her desk there was that awful red plastic flower in a pot, which danced if you clapped near it. So unprofessional!

'So the tablets haven't really helped?' John finally managed to get a word in.

'I'm so sorry but no. In fact, I'd say they haven't made any difference at all, other than make me feel odd.' Joan was apologetic as though it were her fault. 'I had to stop them a couple of days ago. The oddness has gone but the headaches are the same.'

'That's a shame. Any change in your symptoms?'

'Maybe more persistent.'

'All well at home?'

'Of course.' There was no way she was going to admit to any of those worries.

'Are you sure? And here at work? Yours is a busy job, a lot of stress...'

'Fine, fine.'

'Good. Now, I'd just better check a few things. Your blood pressure, the backs of your eyes, your neck, if I may.'

'Of course, Dr Britton.'

Joan submitted to a quick examination, shutting her mouth tightly as John loomed in towards her face to look at her retinas in case her breath smelled. She noticed the hint of his cologne with approval. Subtle but very pleasant, she thought.

John was able to reassure her. 'That all seems fine. I still don't suspect anything serious here at all. I think we're looking at something called chronic daily headache. I'll give you some information about that so you can understand it better and let's try a different tablet. Would you like that?'

'Oh, please.'

'Hopefully, these should break the cycle of headaches and give you some relief. One, each evening. They might make you a little dry mouthed, possibly a little drowsy to start with but it's a very tiny dose, so all being well, all you'll notice is an improvement. Come and see me again in a fortnight and tell me how you've got on.'

'That sounds wonderful. Thank you so much, doctor.'

'I can refer you to a neurologist, if you'd prefer,' he added as an afterthought.

'No, no, I'm more than happy with what you've advised.'

The printer churned out the prescription, which John signed with his usual illegible flourish. He handed it across to her and she smiled gratefully at him.

'You're so kind, Dr Britton.'

'That's what I'm here for.' He reached out and patted her forearm, reassuringly.

'Thank you. It's so nice to have someone to talk to that I trust. Er, Dr Britton, I'll be nipping out for a sandwich in about an hour. Can I get you something? I know you've a really busy afternoon ahead, so you'll probably not have time to go home for lunch.'

John thought for a moment. 'That would be exceedingly kind of you,

Joan. Thank you.'

'Your favourite? Egg mayo and salad?'

'Perfect, in a brown roll please. Oh, and some plain crisps and a flapjack.'

He fumbled in his pocket for some loose change. 'I'll settle up with you when you get back – is that okay?'

'Of course, that's no problem. I'll be back as soon as I can after my lunch break starts.'

'There's no rush. I've plenty to be getting on with. And thanks again.'

Joan left, delighted to be of help. She could still feel his hand on her arm. Rushing to get back to work, she almost knocked over Miss Chisholm who gave her a filthy stare, narrowing her eyes with suspicion as she rushed past.

Chapter Three

John was the last to arrive in the common room, the customary place for after-surgery coffee and chat, which tended to be a mix of comparing notes, offloading worries and, on a good day, some light relief and banter. Clare was embroiled in what appeared to be a difficult telephone conversation, struggling to get a word in, Ed was sitting with his current registrar, Maya, deep in discussion and Ellie, at her laptop, was typing furiously.

He sighed, looking round at all the feverish activity. Now it was all such constant pressure. There never seemed to be a moment's respite, to draw breath and take stock. He could dimly recall the days when they sat round, chatting, signing a few prescriptions, having a coffee before divvying up the few requests for home visits. Not now. Sometimes he felt as though he was running down a mountainside, trying not to fall over but all the time aware that the wave of molten lava behind him, which would surely in the fullness of time engulf him, was getting closer and closer.

More often than not, these days, he no longer looked forward to coming to work. Once upon a time he woke eager to be up and back at his desk, on metaphorical starting blocks, agog to see what surprises and challenges the day held, but not any more. The emphasis had shifted from patient-centred care, which was surely integral to the job, to box ticking, fighting to preserve income, targets, targets and more targets. With huge reluctance, he toed the line, trying to pull his weight and be an equal amongst his partners, for whom he had the utmost respect and affection. They seemed more ready to adopt change, more resilient than him. The benefits of youth. The very worst that might happen was for one of them to turn round and accuse him of falling behind. It simply would not be fair. As senior partner he was supposed to lead by example, but that was so hard when he was so disillusioned. His original intention had been to stay until his sixty-fifth birthday, or longer if possible but now sixty seemed much more attractive and from a financial viewpoint, it was a viable option. He grieved for the job that once was. Change was inevitable, that had to be accepted, but this so-called progress, as he was assured it was, he believed was just change for change's sake and had ensured that general practice would never be the same again.

Having logged out from the computer on his desk downstairs only minutes ago, he slumped into a chair and switched on his laptop to try to make some inroads into his to-do list. No rest for the wicked. Ellie, with her usual intuition, was instantly aware that her partner was not his usual, chirpy self and left her work to make him a cup of coffee, to his specifications – strong, very strong with the merest swirl of milk. She gently placed the mug, full of what looked like unpleasant puddle water, on the table beside him and tactfully moved the biscuit tin out of his reach.

Clare replaced the receiver and growled. 'Why won't some people listen? They ring wanting advice but then when it isn't what they want to hear, they start ranting and raving.'

The others looked suitably sympathetic. They'd all had experiences like that, frustrating and demoralising. The only way to deal with them was to write up good notes and then move on. 'Don't let the buggers get you down,' was one of John's favourite pieces of his advice, which he found hard to take on board personally.

Clare was looking tired, John noticed. Presumably another bad night with her young son, Tom, who was re-writing the text books about sleeping problems. She'd wanted a child for so long and struggled with her pregnancy so that if there were any justice, she ought to be having it easy now. She looked as though she had been to bed in her clothes as they were full of creases. What had happened to her smart tailored frocks and suits? Now all she seemed to wear were loose-fitting tops over shapeless trousers to hide the weight she still had to lose. Knowing her well, John knew that if he asked if there were any problems, she would rapidly reply in the negative, never one to admit defeat of any sort, often at the expense of her own wellbeing. Perhaps a better way of approaching her would be through Ellie, who was a close friend and who seemed to be able to permeate the tough exterior and find out the truth. Either way, they all needed to support her more, if she'd let them.

'Bad morning?' asked Ellie, sitting down beside him, crossing her slender legs and helping herself to a chocolate digestive which she tried to hide.

John half smiled and nodded. 'There's so much administration work to do, I constantly feel I haven't got time to do what I'm best at – talking to and looking after my patients. How can we possibly consult properly in ten minutes? When I first started in this job, patients came in with one problem, now they come in with four or five and expect me to sort out all of them there and then.'

'We all feel the same, John,' Ellie agreed empathically. 'Last week I had someone with a list of thirteen things they wanted to discuss. I wanted to scream! Is there anything I can do today to help? I've only got three home visits. I could rattle round them and come back and help with duty doctor surgery, if you like.'

'Don't worry, I'll be fine. You've more than enough of your own work to be doing, but thanks. I appreciate the offer.' He grimaced. 'It's just one of those days. Early morning surgery, duty doctor surgery and long afternoon surgery. No time to go home for lunch and, oh, to finish with, a meeting with the receptionists and Elliott. I'll not be home before eight, I don't suppose. Barely time to turn round before it's time to come back again. I might as well just sleep on my examination couch.'

Chapter Four

Switching on her television, Joan sank into an armchair and placed her mug of tea and supper on the little table beside her. What a day she had had! Late home because of a receptionists' meeting, chaired by Elliot, she had been relieved to find that her mother had fed Simeon and persuaded him to go to bed, a remarkable achievement by anyone's standards. Shame that they had left her the washing up, though. An unappetising smell of stale fried food greeted her, probably sausages and chips as fat was congealing in the frying pan on the cooker. On the table, still in its wrapper, was a half eaten Battenberg cake, squashed out of shape and looking rather sorry for itself.

The meeting had not been particularly enjoyable. Too many changes had been promised at work and Joan wasn't entirely convinced that they were for the better. The two younger receptionists, Gary and Gemma, wanted a more modern uniform, from an upmarket store rather than the catalogue they traditionally used and Gemma wanted trousers – unheard of. Elizabeth, predictably, had sat nodding her head, agreeing with everyone, afraid to voice her opinion for fear of confrontation.

When she had first started the job, Joan had worn a white coat, like the doctors used to, which she had chastely buttoned up to the neck and she so enjoyed the feeling of dominance that it gave her. Now of course, it was all about pretty blouses, bright colours and cosy cardigans. She didn't approve but pretended to so as not to antagonise her staff or Elliot. So long as her uniform was slightly different, setting her apart from the rest, that was all that mattered.

Next, a new computer system was promised for next year. Well, that would be a nightmare, what with the learning involved and trying to keep the place running smoothly, simultaneously.

The annual pay increase, on which she depended, hung in the balance as overall, practice profits were not even static but falling and there was to be a newsletter for the patients.

Joan had left work feeling unsettled, close to agitated if she were honest, and to have been greeted by a shouting match with Simeon would have been the final straw. Nowadays he had no problem voicing his opinions very loudly be they about bedtime, supper snacks, or video games versus homework. He really was at a very difficult age, she decided but then shuddered at the thought that there were infinitely more difficult stages lying ahead.

For now, though, he was asleep or feigning sleep which was good enough for her, even though the latter was more likely. She considered going into his room to check but it was fast approaching the start of one of her favourite soaps and then there was the hospital drama straight after and then that comedy programme which was a bit near the knuckle but still worth a look. She was badly in need of some relaxation time before bed and the start of another day.

Biting into her ham sandwich, she realised how hungry she was. Once that was eaten, she'd get a piece of the cake and then open the box of chocolates that one of the patients had handed in for Dr Jennings but that somehow Joan had forgotten to pass on. Dr Jennings received a lot of gifts from grateful patients so one fewer would surely go unnoticed and, anyway, she should set an example and eat the healthy diet she was always going on about.

Ivy was half asleep on the sofa, head lolling inelegantly to one side, disturbing the white wispy hair that had been forced into tight curls by the next-door neighbour's daughter, Belle, who wanted to be a hairdresser. The hair was so thin now that it was impossible not to stare at the pink scalp on show. Ivy's blouse had become open at the top and untucked at the bottom to reveal a greying petticoat and a yellowing wool vest. Joan gazed at her with a mixture of guilt and sadness. It really was too much to ask her to look after Simeon as much as she did. She had to face up to reality – that Ivy was getting old and worn out, physically and mentally. Little occurrences of late had planted the seeds of suggestion in her mind that Ivy was starting with a form of dementing illness. Her short-term memory was deteriorating, lists of reminders were stuck everywhere – in the kitchen, by the telephone, on the front and back doors but milk would still end up in anywhere other than the fridge, jobs would not get done and Simeon, with his customary lack of diplomacy, was forever moaning that his lunch box was sandwich-less, or the sandwiches missing their filling, guffawing as he did so at her indiscretions and mistakes. And if that was hard to handle, worst of all were the irrefutable signs that her personal hygiene was not what it used to be. Sheets were too frequently blowing in the breeze when Joan came home, Ivy's desperate attempt to conceal nocturnal accidents, and the laundry basket always seemed full of her underwear.

Joan had no option though. None of her acquaintances could be asked to help out any more and the neighbours had experienced enough of her son to say no and turn away rapidly, if approached. After school club had politely, but firmly, excluded him after an incident involving one of the music teachers, a fire extinguisher and a video posted on social media, so however she looked at it, Joan was completely dependent on her mother Ivy.

It was instantly apparent to anyone who met her that Ivy worshipped her grandson and, in his own peculiar way, her feelings were recip-rocated. During his short life, Simeon had quickly learned that his grandmother was a soft touch; that she was happy to negotiate for the sake of an easy life and everything had its price. Joan was aware that money changed hands on a regular but one-way basis and this was the mainstay of Simeon's good behaviour. She did not approve but as it helped to ease a potentially explosive situation, she was prepared to turn a blind eye and pretend she was totally oblivious to what was going on. Time and again she told herself that what he really needed was a father figure in his life, someone to rein him in, teach him some boundaries and introduce a hefty helping of discipline to each day. Ivy had never been and would never be able to do this and Simeon rejoiced in this fact.

Ivy grunted as the television came to life and opened her eyes. For a moment she looked lost, unsure where she was but quickly became orientated and turned to her daughter.

'Hello, love. Good day? You're late.'

'The usual. I told you about the meeting. Did you forget? I did write down a reminder for you.'

'No, of course not.' Ivy had no insight into her problem and a penchant for excuses. 'Just a bit sleepy, that's all.'

'How's Simeon been?'

'Oh, he's fine. He's been as good as gold. Fast asleep as soon as his head touched the pillow. Said he had cross-country running today but he hid in the bushes until it was over! What's he like? He needed some money for a school project, so I've sorted that out. Only ten pounds. Can I get you anything?'

Joan pointed to her plate of sandwiches as she imagined the ten pounds being spent on junk food and comics. 'I'm sorted, thanks. Kettle's just boiled if you want a cuppa. No, you stop there and I'll get it for you. You'll have had a busy day too.'

'Well, I need a pee before our programme starts.'

Ivy rearranged herself on the sofa into a sitting position, before heaving her body upright. The effort was considerable. 'Oops!' she confessed, a look of horror on her face as she grabbed herself between the legs. 'Better dash!'

Joan sighed and, once her mother had left the room, went over to the sofa and felt the cushions. Thank goodness, no damp patch, just the stale odour of age having occupied that seat all day. Joan would need to suggest, again, that Ivy changed her clothes a little more regularly and tried wearing the pads she had tactfully bought for her.

Looking around the room, Joan wished there was the money to decorate. It was well overdue. Never mind shabby chic or whatever people called it, her house was simply shabby. Walls that had once been creamy-white and fresh now looked grubby, the fireplace was old fashioned, ugly and dusty, the carpet stained by more spills than she cared to remember and the three-piece suite was almost a four-piece suite, it was so dilapidated. Not a lot to show for years of hard work. But then reception work had never paid well. Once the food had been paid for along with the basic bills, there was precious little left for niceties such as new furniture or colour-coordinated curtains.

Still, the one interesting thing at the meeting was that the idea had been mooted for them to have a newsletter, to pass information on to the patients and encourage them to take more responsibility for their own health. The suggestion was a page on the practice website and then also a paper copy to be handed out at reception and left in the waiting areas.

Her initial reaction had been one of disdain. The touchy-feely approach was becoming all too common at the surgery for her liking.

However, this did create an opportunity to shine and Joan felt confident that this was a job she could perform with aplomb and one for which she might be able to negotiate a little bonus if she did it really proficiently. Definitely something to be looked into further and with her spotless track record it was probably a done deal that the editorial position was hers. She made a mental note to speak to Elliott the next day but she needed to come up with some compelling argument to prove her worth.

So while the television droned on, rather than be swept away by the machinations of the characters who usually gripped her attention, she started jotting down ideas in a little note book. Obviously, health information, reminders about the flu jab, advice for new parents, but it was imperative that it was written for the patients, to catch their eyes and make them want to read it all. Healthy recipes, maybe? Puzzles? Profiles about the staff members would be good. The partners, nurses,

Elliot, herself of course and maybe some of her reception colleagues, if she felt it appropriate. Pleased with and liking her ideas, she turned her attention back to the television, the gory entrails of a road traffic accident victim and the cellophane wrapping around the chocolates.

Halfway through the lower layer and after a further thirty minutes of the complex interpersonal relationships of her favourite heroine, Ivy was nodding again and Joan's head was thumping. While the adverts were on, she rummaged in her handbag for the new tablets she had been prescribed. Thinking back to the time Dr Britton had spent with her, she smiled. He had been so kind and understanding. Reassuring too because, yes, the headaches did frighten her sometimes. Mostly she accepted that they were stress related and worse when she was tired out or Simeon was at his least endearing but occasionally, if they were really bad and she felt compelled to go and lie down, then visions of strokes and burst blood vessels did rear up in front of her eyes. Dr Britton seemed to know all this without being told. He had even patted her hand and told her not to worry. Little wonder he was so popular with his patients. He understood how they felt. And he had asked her to go back in a couple of weeks. None of this 'come back if it doesn't improve' line of dismissal that was all too common these days; no, he wanted to see her either way. Consideration such as this was over and above his job description, she felt sure. Maybe it was because she was a valued member of staff or maybe, just maybe, he simply liked her. She definitely liked seeing him.

Chapter Five

Elliott Douglas had been practice manager for years, starting not long after John had become a partner. He had started out in hospital administration but, having reached as far in the ranks as he wanted to go, thought that a sideways step into the confused and perpetual motion that was community medicine would challenge and refresh him. He had not been disappointed. If anything, it had exceeded his expectations and the mixture of enjoyment and commitment plus his exacting personality were a recipe for outstanding success. The four partners relied heavily on him as he had taken over all the running of the business in his brusque and no-nonsense way, thus leaving them to follow his order to 'get on and look after the patients'. Not one to suffer fools, he liked to run a tight ship. He had a sixth sense which informed him when there were any ripples of discontent among the ranks, which earned him the dubious accolade of being psychic or alternatively suspected of having bugged the building.

Joan was sitting opposite him. She was feeling extremely well, her headache having gone overnight. Elliott noticed that there was a flush to her cheeks and that she was having trouble sitting still, a far cry from her more predictable frowning face designed to cast terror into patients' hearts. More times than he cared to remember, particularly of late, he had tried to persuade Joan to soften her approach somewhat, without success. She looks almost pretty today, he thought, with her dark brown hair held back in a clasp at the nape of her neck and some subtle but enhancing make-up that she did not normally condone.

'So you want to edit the newsletter, do you, Joan?'

'Yes, please, I'm sure this is something I can do well. I've already had all sorts of ideas and even thought of a name for it – *The Teviotdale Telegraph*.' She referred to her notebook and proceeded to itemise them. 'I think it's vital that we don't make it too complicated and find snippets to put in that will catch the eye and be interesting. If we have some of those, then people will want to read the rest, which can be about health care, medical new, advice tips of common ailments – all that sort of stuff.' Joan looked up.

Elliott nodded slowly, twiddling his Biro in one hand.

'I think you have a good point there, Joan. I also think that you're in a very good position to do this. As our head receptionist, you see both sides of the practice – the patients and the doctors. But have you time to do it? I know you've a lot on at home and this work would almost certainly have to be done in your spare time. I can't afford to let you off any other duties.'

'I wouldn't expect that. I'm sure I can manage. Once my son is in bed, I've a few hours every evening, plus weekends of course.'

Elliott tapped on his upper right incisor as he considered before putting his Biro down neatly.

'Okay, let's give it a go. Can you have the first copy ready for me in, say, a week? For me to read through and then if I like it, I'll pass it round the partners for the final approval. How about that?'

Joan beamed from ear to ear. A rare event. 'That's perfect. You won't be disappointed, I promise. I'll start straightaway.'

Elliott nodded 'Good! I shall look forward to seeing it. Don't make the mistake of trying to make it too long. See if you can get some of the others to contribute. Remember, we want to produce this on a monthly basis, so this has to be sustainable.'

'Of course, I understand. I'd also thought of having a suggestion box on the front desk, so patients can let us know what they'd like too.' She paused, biting her top lip, suddenly serious but felt brave enough to continue. 'I just wondered...'

'Yes, Joan?'

'Is there any way there might be a little extra money for doing it? I mean, I will be doing it in my own time.'

Elliott considered her, not unkindly. 'Let's see how you get on to start with, shall we? I can't make any promises at this stage. Reception runs on a shoestring as it is.'

Joan tried not to look too disappointed. She supposed it hadn't been an outright 'no', so there was some hope. It was up to her now, to show them that what she contributed to *TheTeviotdale Telegraph* was worth a bonus.

She knew exactly what she wanted to do first.

John was in his consulting room, catching up with telephone calls and letters in a lackadaisical and inefficient way, which annoyed him, as he liked to feel on top of his workload. He thought he might concentrate better in here, rather than go up to the common room where there would be the inevitable distractions of other people, the kettle and the lure of the biscuit tin. He chose to ignore the fact that he was now a type 2 diabetic and took solace from the fact that his blood results were only just into the abnormal range, which was of course, an approach, which if taken by one of his patients, he would have castigated immediately. A few months ago he had started peeing too often and getting up in the night several times to do the same, wondered about his prostate gland but all his tests had come back normal, apart from the one for diabetes. His mother had been diabetic in later life and his older brother also was, so he supposed it was no great surprise but even then did not want to admit it had happened to him. Rather than rush onto lots of prescribed medication, he had persuaded Ellie, who had broken the bad news to him, to let him have a really good try on a healthy diet, lose a stone in weight and start walking more. He was hopeful that this recipe would also have a beneficial effect on his blood pressure which was a little high. But when work was bad, or if he missed a meal, biscuits or a chocolate bar were a quick fix and who in their right mind would go to the bother of eating a proper meal when time was of the essence and the first patient of the next surgery was due in less than half an hour. Faye, his wife, did her best. His evening meals and breakfasts were always balanced and nutritionally perfect but even she was unable to watch over him twenty-four hours a day.

He dreaded the thought of what he called 'being medicalised'. Turning from a person into a patient, having multiple repeat prescriptions, one drug for one condition, another to prevent something else, a third to deal with side-effects of the first and so it went on. In his heart, he knew he would have to acquiesce in the future but not yet, surely.

Defiantly, he bit into a large piece of Bakewell tart, which he had stopped and bought from the local cafe and delicatessen, Delicious, famed for its large portions of more-ish home-baking.

A soft tap at his open door mercifully diverted his thoughts. Hurriedly and not without some guilt, he pushed his cake back into the bag and hid it in the top drawer of his desk. Joan's neat little face was peering at him. He hoped passionately that it wasn't another house call or anything that demanded any effort. He simply did not have the energy for anything extra today.

'Yes, Joan,' he started, a resigned tone to his voice, reflexively wiping his mouth in case of stray crumbs.

'Sorry to bother you, Dr Britton, but may I bob in for a moment please?' She sounded suspiciously chirpy.

'Of course. How can I help? Is there a problem with the tablets I gave you yesterday?' He had slipped back into his role of doctor. So much easier.

'No, no, far from it. I've taken one and it's been brilliant.'

'Well, that's great. Keep on taking them and I'll see you as planned.'

Joan digested this advice, before arranging herself on the chair, pulling it a little closer as this was a chat and not an official consultation.

'Elliott's agreed to let me write the newsletter,' she whispered, conspiratorially.

John nodded slowly, wondering what on earth she was talking about until a vague recollection of the receptionists' meeting came to him.

'So,' she inhaled deeply for maximum effect, 'one of my ideas, which I think you'll like, is to write a small piece about individuals in the practice. A different person each month. An almost light-hearted question and answer session. I'm sure you know the sort of thing. Like they have on the penultimate pages of magazines.'

John continued to nod, wondering where this was going.

'I'd like to start with you, please. As senior partner, it seems only fitting.'

John rapidly switched to shaking his head, with some vigour. He raised his hands.

'Oh, Joan, I don't know. Perhaps it'd be better to start with yourself, as it's your newsletter, or with Elliott, as practice manager.'

Joan's mind, however, was made up. 'No, I think you'd be perfect. I'll do Elliott later and I'm sure no one wants to read about me, when they can read about you instead.'

She smiled, coaxingly.

John pulled a face, far from convinced. 'It's not really my sort of thing, Joan. I'd rather my patients didn't know too much about me, if I'm honest. It's bad enough living in a small market town like Lambdale and not being able to move without someone spotting you.'

'Nonsense. I'm not going to be writing anything salacious or revealing. This isn't a Sunday tabloid. Just a few little details. I'll let you read through it when it's done.'

One final attempt to deflect her advances. 'I've house calls to do.'

'No, you haven't!' Joan was triumphant. 'I've divided all the calls up between the others and said you had an urgent meeting to attend, so you've plenty of time.'

'Joan, you shouldn't have done that!'

'Oh. Don't you worry. There were only a handful. Just the usual stuff – chest infections and dreary conditions like that. So, may I start? I won't take up much of your valuable time...'

He had no alternative but to agree.

Joan flicked open a little notebook that she produced from one pocket and a pen from another. She sat up, ramrod straight and rather in the manner of a very new constable preparing to take a statement. She cleared her throat.

'Thank you for agreeing to be interviewed, Dr Britton. Now, to start with, tell me how long you have been at the practice?'

So her questions began. From revealing the fact that he had been born not far from Southampton to telling her that his favourite dessert was fresh fruit salad (it was actually treacle sponge and custard but he thought that didn't sound very healthy), he steadily supplied her with answers to all her searching questions. Yes, he had had a very happy childhood and university, yes it was true that he won the paediatrics prize in his fourth year and yes, he loved all animals, particularly dogs. His ideal day would be spent with his wife and family, at the seaside, walking along the beach and then having fish and chips out of newspaper, his favourite colour was blue and his preferred tipple was a large cup of Yorkshire tea or some sparkling water (another small white lie). He declined to tell her what he gave Faye for her last birthday or what she gave him, despite Joan's insistence that the readers would love to know. There was only so much he was prepared to divulge.

'Perfect! Thank you so much, Dr Britton. That was fascinating. I bet there are requests for a sequel! Now, one last thing,' she reached into her bag and John wondered what was coming next.

'A photo!' she announced, producing her mobile phone and switching it on. 'There must be a lovely photo of you at the start of the article. Smile please! I said smile...'

John started to object but she carried on regardless, snapping away, moving around to catch him at what she referred to as 'his best angle', insisting on a little grin here, a serious look there, so she had lots to choose from.

'Surely that's enough?' he suggested.

'Not quite...and a few with your glasses off, please...'

More snapping.

'Lovely! I'll definitely be able to find something from that lot.'

Pushing her chair back to the correct position for a patient and scooping up her notebook, Joan rose to leave. 'You're looking tired today, if you don't mind me saying.'

John shrugged and put on his best smile. 'Just some worries over patients.'

'You poor soul. You're always so thoughtful. Shall I get you a coffee?'

'That'd be most kind. Nice and strong please. No sugar.'

'Won't be more than a couple of ticks! Tell you what; I'll see if I can find some biccies as well.'

The interview had gone so much better than she had hoped. He had really opened up to her, told her things that nobody else knew and only she had seen the way he had looked at her while he had done so. He really was remarkably handsome.

John's afternoon went better. Funnily enough, maybe the break from house calls and that ridiculous chat with Joan had helped clear his mind. He had rung home and spoken to Faye, who had reminded him that she was playing tennis later and that his supper was ready to be popped into the oven. She also made him promise not to eat cake and ice cream for pudding. The sound of her voice, even when admonitory, made him feel better.

His patients were more straightforward and undemanding. Finishing near enough on time, he felt the most upbeat he had in a long while as he cleared his desk, rattled off a couple of very quick two-line referral letters and a report to the local housing office, firstly describing the deplorable flat an elderly couple were forced to live in and secondly making no bones about the fact that something must be done and as soon as humanly possible. In his experience, doctors' letters rarely carried any weight with these sorts of matters but he felt better for knowing that he had tried his best.

Ed's face appeared around his door. 'We're going for a quick drink at the pub. Fancy joining us?'

John accepted, being in no rush to get home. Bidding good night to Joan and Elizabeth, he walked up the lane and across the market square, where stall-holders were packing up for the day, battling with their canvas booths against the gusty wind. Chatting to Clare and Ellie, Ed having gone on ahead, he thought, thank goodness for the three of them. They were not simply work colleagues, partners in business but good friends too.

Their usual table was free and they sat down as Ed arrived with their drinks, red wine for Ellie and John (a token nod to his so-called healthy diet), white wine for Clare and a pint of local brew for Ed.

'Cheers,' they agreed, in unison, raising their glasses. 'Here's to the completion of another successful day!'

Chapter Six

Laden with three carrier bags of shopping which kept bashing against her legs and snagging her tights – her last remaining decent pair – Joan wearily reached home, longing for a cup of tea, only to find Simeon at his worst and Ivy looking completely bewildered. The noise from some violent computer game was audible from the pavement; the curtains were still open and the milk bottles still on the doorstep, one silver top savaged by some birds. Weeds were gradually taking over the gravel but Joan had far too many other jobs to do before sorting that out. Needless to say, she had asked, or rather bribed Simeon to do it for her, but he had screamed some unsavoury words at her and run up to his room, slamming all the doors as he went.

She opened the door and thankfully let the bags slump onto the floor. The ruckus was so loud that it made her eardrums hurt. Blood-curdling screams and repeated gunfire confirmed her fears that this game was totally unsuitable for a nine year old. Wondering where he had got it from but knowing where the money had come from, Joan walked into the lounge and sat down heavily. Ivy smiled vacantly at her while Simeon, far too engrossed, ignored her completely.

What a welcome, she thought.

'Have you had tea?' Joan bellowed, over the din.

'No dear. We thought we'd wait for you as we knew you were shopping.'

Fabulous, Joan sighed. The last thing I needed. I wanted to get started on the newsletter, type up Dr Britton's interview and choose the best photo but now I can't until I've fed us all.

'Why don't you come and help me, Simmy? We can chat about what we've done today,' she suggested only to be rewarded by a blank stare. 'I think you've played enough of that dreadful game now. You'll have nightmares, you know you will.'

'I won't. No! Don't turn it off. No! Mum! Stop it! Give me back the remote. Now!'

But Joan had snatched it from him and ignoring his increasingly foul-mouthed objections, switched over to a gentle comedy for Ivy and marched into the tiny, cramped kitchen, picking up her shopping from the hall on her way. She had bought lamb chops for supper. They hadn't been cheap but she'd seen them and really fancied a change from the perpetual rotation of pizza, frozen fish, sausages and then a roast on Sunday. With hindsight, it had been a foolish and impulsive buy. She knew that. Simeon would refuse to eat them, complain he didn't like bones and sit and sulk until she made him pizza with extra cheese (more reason to have nightmares) and Ivy would look apologetically at her and make excuses on the grounds that her teeth weren't what they used to be. Anxious to avoid any squabbles and get Simeon off to bed as soon as possible, Joan put two chops under the grill for herself, a pizza and a baking tray loaded with chips in the oven and opened a cardboard packet of boil-in-the-bag cod in parsley sauce for Ivy. Why did one meal have to be so complicated?

They ate supper off plates on their laps, not bothering to chat, silenced by the television. By permitting a game show that involved a lot of slapstick and canned laughter, Simeon sat relatively still, eating noisily with his mouth wide open, only pausing when someone fell over and got splattered with green goo. Joan's one request that he might pay a little more attention to his meal and chew more quietly, keeping his mouth closed, inevitably resulted in the opposite. All she longed for was for him to be upstairs and in bed. Then she'd be able to get on with the newsletter.

A far less enthusiastic diner was Ivy, who picked at her fish

29

disinterestedly, flicking the tiny specks of parsley to one side of her plate.

'Something wrong, Mum?' asked Joan.

'It's a bit cold,' she commented, 'and this sauce is too rich for me. I'll be up all night with the burps.'

'I'm sorry. I did rush a bit. Shall I heat it up for you?'

'Don't worry, I'll do my best.' Ivy uttered a martyr-like sigh. 'You enjoy yours. You'll be hungry after your long day. It's so lovely to have you home. We've been quite lonely today, haven't we, Simeon?'

'No.'

Ivy chuckled. 'Isn't he a laugh? I think he'll be a comedian when he grows up.'

Simeon smirked. 'Thanks, Grandma. Oh, by the way, you haven't forgotten that five pounds you promised me, have you?'

'Did I, dear?' Ivy looked puzzled.

'Yes, Grandma. For school books. Oh, you're always forgetting things. Good job I'm here to remind you.'

Joan looked from one to the other, instantly suspicious. In this day and age, you didn't buy school books, let alone for five pounds.

Ivy pushed aside her plate, fish largely untouched, and reached for her capacious but nearly empty old and battered handbag.

'Of course I remember! Just testing you! Got to keep you young ones on your toes! Five pounds did you say?'

She snapped open the clasp on her purse and pulled out a ten-pound note.

'This is all I have. You'd better take it and if there's any left over you can give it back to me.'

'Of course, Grandma,' beamed Simeon sycophantically. 'You don't mind if I buy a few sweets as well though, do you? You know how hungry I get...'

Ivy shook her head. 'Get on with you! Get some sweets and a bar of chocolate for me and one for your mum, but no more of those horrible noisy games. All right? You're the best grandson an old lady like me could ask for. Come and give me a kiss.'

Much to Joan's amazement, Simeon did get up and kiss his grandmother on the cheek, with touching tenderness, not a quick peck out of duty. The moment was spoiled as he pocketed the money and returned to his pizza, winding loops of cheese around his tongue in a disgusting way, happy that his mission was accomplished. Had she, Joan, asked for a show of affection, his response would have been 'ugh' as he turned away. Maybe though, there was some hope.

It was infinitely quicker for Joan to clear up on her own. Left to her own devices, she washed dirty pots and plates from supper, lunch and breakfast, leaving them to dry in a teetering pile. She scrubbed at a couple of mugs, badly tannin stained but gave up and instead set about tidying up as best as possible, wiping up crumbs and smears of jam and dropping cold, damp teabags into the overflowing bin, which nobody ever thought of emptying apart from her. As usual, it was full to bursting.

Girding her loins, she went back into the lounge, ready to start the long debate with Simeon on the subject of going to bed. The promise of chocolate if he went for a bath immediately and then was allowed to read before putting his light out worked, once he had checked out how big the bar was. Ivy went up with him, to run his bath, turn down his covers and fetch a cardigan as she was feeling chilly. Joan was able to hear the two of them chatting, quite civilly and wondered why on earth she couldn't do the same. In many ways, Ivy had replaced her as Simeon's mother. Ivy was always there, provided nourishment and love and erroneously smothered him with favours and treat. Joan felt like an outsider. Some days she felt like a lodger in her own home, walking on eggshells lest she upset him and having to bear the indignity of the two of them ganging up against her, most of the time. There was no option. She could not afford to be at home more than she was unless she found a new, better- paid job where her hours were fewer. The chances of this were slim, verging on zero; she knew that and anyway she was moderately happy at the practice, working for pleasant people. That was why, if there was the slightest chance of a pay rise for doing the newsletter, she must not miss out.

Ivy returned, minus cardigan and had to be reminded to go and get it. Leaving her to choose her evening's viewing, Joan set up the laptop she had been allowed to bring home from work for the purposes of the newsletter on what was at one time the dining table but now tended to be a place to dump anything and everything, rather than find a proper storing space. One day soon, she would get round to having a really good clear out.

For once, she was so preoccupied by what she was doing that Joan ignored the television completely, losing track of time and was astounded when Ivy announced that it was bedtime and was her daughter going to be much longer?

'It's not right, you having to work all day for that place and then all evening too. You've barely stopped tapping that thing for hours,' was her verdict.

'It's fine, Mum. I offered to do it. I'm really enjoying it so far. I had no idea that was the time. You go on up and I'll just do a little bit more and then finish for the day. Another early start tomorrow. I'll be glad when the weekend comes.'

'If you're sure. I'll go on up and check on Simeon on my way.'

'Thanks. Oh, Mum? Please stop giving him money all the time. Next time he asks you, discuss it with me first.'

Ivy gave her a look. 'I've no other grandchildren to spoil.' Joan winced internally. 'He's a good lad really. He loves his grandma. Good night.'

As part of her routine, Ivy switched off the main light, leaving Joan in the glow of the laptop screen. Saving her most recent paragraph, she reviewed the work she had completed with satisfaction. A lot of humdrum stuff about opening hours and out of hours cover, tips on how to self-medicate coughs and colds and some healthy recipes using lentils and split peas. She had headlined these as 'Taking your Pulse', loving the association with the heart beat and feeling sure she had tapped into a previously unknown way of reaching the general public.

The interview with Dr Britton was tremendous. It painted him exactly as he was, compassionate, gentle and intelligent, traits which were backed up by any of the photos she had taken, apart from one that was blurred because he had moved. So engrossed had she been that she hadn't realised how many questions she had ended up asking him or how much space it would fill in the newsletter. She re-read what she had written a dozen times and pondered over the photos. What an exceptional man. So busy perpetually, but he still had time for her and if she wasn't mistaken, there were deeper reasons for this.

She had found out so much about him that some editing was necessary, sadly. Still, she didn't want everyone to know as much about him as she did. She tidied up her article a little, in a way she felt sure he would approve of as what she did was erase any mention at all of his wife and family. That bit really was irrelevant.

Chapter Seven

John was buttering his toast, carefully and deliberately taking care with each corner, hoping that if he moved in slow motion then the clock might follow suit. Another tediously long day stretched ahead, surgery, home visits, then lunchtime taken up with yet another staff meeting and finally the afternoon as duty doctor, with the responsibility of seeing all the urgent cases – most of which weren't, fielding endless telephone calls and sorting out test results, messages and letters. The very thought of it all made him feel vaguely nauseous. Where had all these meetings come from? Now every moment of his day was being encroached upon, squeezing what he considered to be his real job into insufficient hours to perform satisfactorily. He helped himself to a large dollop of marmalade, which he noted, with a sneer, was clearly marked as 'low sugar –suitable for diabetics'.

Faye was watching him, a worried frown on her normally sanguine face. It upset her to see the change that had taken place over the last ten years or so. Gone was the man who was out of the house with a bounce in his step and who returned, leaving his work behind him – more or less – and now instead she was living with someone who was shrouded in a cloak of gloom and occasionally despair. He always perked up as the weekend approached and Friday mornings were a rather different kettle of fish as this was also his half day – one of the perks, of which there were miserably few – of being senior partner. But as the weekend passed, she could almost see him shrinking in size and being enveloped again in a black cloud. Initially she had seen this starting on Sunday evening, after dinner, when he sat down with a large whisky and pretended to watch television but then it began to be the afternoon, then as soon as he woke and now, he started to fight with it on Saturday evening. He brought more work home with him now and also had some means of logging in to work from home which meant that he was always checking, finishing something off, agonising over an audit, writing up notes for his annual appraisal. Without fail, there was some work to be done in some shape or form.

So many changes had taken place in general practice that now his job description bore little resemblance to the one he had originally signed up for. Back in those days, the emphasis was on the word 'general' and John delighted in the fact that from one hour to the next he never knew what was coming to challenge him. He might be driving off to deliver a baby at the local GP-run maternity hospital (now closed and turned into holiday flats), visiting someone convalescing at the cottage hospital (also now closed and turned into a boutique bed and breakfast), stitching up a patient after a minor operation (no longer funded) or visiting a terminally ill patient (now taken over more or less by the palliative care team, leaving him feeling on the periphery and excluded). No matter how much he protested, aspects of his job were being claimed by others, robbing him of the joy and interest he loved and leaving him with seemingly endless days of sitting on his backside in front of a computer.

Faye was doing her best, as she always did, constantly trying to cheer him up, find positives in life, encouraging him to make the most of his holidays and keep work and home separate. The diagnosis of diabetes had coincided with their youngest son buying a house in Portsmouth and leaving home. Both these events had shaken him badly.

'It happens to patients, not to me,' he had wailed when he broke the news to her. 'I don't want aspirin every day, I don't want a statin because I'm not convinced of the benefit, I don't want metformin because it might give me side effects.'

'Darling, you're only human too,' she had tried to appease him, giving him a hug. 'Let's try really really hard with diet, some weight loss and exercise as Ellie suggested. It might be all that you need for a few years.'

He was not convinced but went along with her plans, sensing a temporary lifeline.

It was constantly at the back on his mind. Way back he had worked on a medical ward where the consultants in charge specialised in diabetes. Rarely required to go to the out-patient clinic, his view of the condition was totally skewed towards the patients with severe complications. Blocked circulation leading to amputations, heart disease, stroke, and loss of eyesight – all such a terrifying and humiliating prospect. Even now, after three decades in general practice, being involved in the other end of the spectrum and aware that millions of diabetics were living normal lives, holding down normal jobs and taking control of their condition as best they could, it was far too easy for him to be transported back to the horrors of that ward and the sights he saw.

Faye knew all this, even though he rarely brought the subject up. His large portions of pudding were merely acts of defiance. Soon, he would come to accept his new way of life, she hoped, but until then, discussing the topic resulted in circuitous conversations that achieved nothing but general disgruntledness.

Stereotypically, they had met through work. Faye had been a nurse on the paediatric ward when John was working there for six months of his training. What had impressed him first were her unflappability and her flair to cope with everything and anything and make it look easy. While he was completely terrified of handling the tiny babies, let alone perform any investigations on them, Faye gave the impression that it came naturally to her. Nearly all the little patients stopped crying in her presence (John noticed he tended to have the opposite effect) and it had not taken intelligence of genius level to work out that if you wanted to get on well on the ward, she was a good person to have on your side. He was a quick learner, loving the work, and rapidly became a valued member of the team, so asking her out for a drink had been a natural progression and one that, after a slightly stuttering start, resulted in them spending increasing amounts of time together, not just on the ward, and falling in love.

Devotedly, she had followed him where his training took him, sharing accommodation of varying degrees of comfort, giving birth to their first son and house training their first Springer spaniel puppy, until he applied for and was offered the partnership in Lambdale. Then they had been able to look for a home, somewhere to put down roots, plan a larger family, and become part of a community. For many years this had been the case; Faye had been the dependable woman behind the successful GP, juggling the home, family and growing number of pets as well as playing tennis, wrestling with the art of flower arranging and taking on a major role fund-raising for a local charity that rescued and re-homed unwanted dogs and cats. John joined her on the tennis court at weekends and on summer evenings if he was able, where they played their best but never quite managed to get further than the semi-finals of the Lambdale Tennis Club Championships, apart from one year when it was by default rather than sporting prowess.

Like a malignancy, John's work began to erode into his personal life. Subtly at first but with a steady relentless pressure which showed no signs of letting up. Initially he laughed it off, determined to ignore it and let nothing change his idyllic way of life but it became an increasingly uphill battle as the relentless change and stress began to take over. The children were growing up too, no longer full of chat and fun, clamouring for his attention, but more often than not, hiding away in their rooms, sullen and uncommunicative, ostensibly working while listening to cacophonous music which John couldn't be bothered to try to understand. Then, just as they were emerging from their adolescent pupae and becoming pleasant people to be around, they went off to university, established their own lives and only paid flying, if regular visits.

Thank goodness for Faye, the constant in his life. Non-judgemental, supportive and, somehow, ever optimistic. How did she manage that? When he looked at her, she was still as beautiful as the first day he had seen her. While he had gone grey and a bit bald, she was still blond (with only a little bit of help from her hairdresser) and her skin looked untouched by the ravages of time.

His toast was finished and Faye had put away the bread, eliminating the chance of another slice that might delay his departure a little longer. But he hated being late more than anything. If he didn't start seeing patients on time, he felt unsynchronised for the entire surgery, so with reluctance, he got up from the table, welcomed the huge hug that Faye gave him and with taut, hunched shoulders, made his way to the car.

Chapter Eight

Seated around the table in the rather dark meeting room (it was at the back of the building and looked out onto a row of trees) were the receptionists, John and Elliot. The original plan for the meeting to be at lunchtime had been scuppered by an unprecedented demand for appointments, resulting in John and Ellie having to do an extra surgery late morning, after house calls. So now it was after seven o'clock and none of them, apart perhaps from Elliott, whose devotion to his job went over and above any standard description, wanted to be there. A long day had passed eventually and everyone was tired out and longing to go home. But Elliott had insisted that there were no opportunities in the near future for this meeting and the best plan was to stay an hour late (with extra pay for their time). He had promised them all that they would be away by seven thirty.

Joan was sitting bolt upright in her chair, watching everyone, including John, who was seated opposite her and whom she thought looked a little weary. She had changed, as had most of them, out of her uniform and was wearing a navy skirt and a pale-blue twinset with smart black flat shoes. He's probably hungry, she decided, aware of her own stomach rumbling. She liked it that he was the partner responsible for the staff and so always attended the meetings. He rarely said anything that wasn't sensible and apposite and it gave her great satisfaction to quote his words when she was dealing with her staff. They really thought along very similar lines.

'...and so onto the newsletter. John, would you like to say a few words?' Elliott's words were rhetorical.

John cleared his throat and took a sip of cold tea from the mug in front of him. It had been a preferable choice to the tap water that was on offer.

'Well,' he began, 'I think congratulations must go to Joan for producing such a professional piece of work. It's evident that you put a lot of time and effort it. Well done!'

He clapped briefly, pointing his hands towards the author of the newsletter.

Joan began to flush.

'I'd second that,' Elliott nodded. 'I have to confess I wasn't sure if you were up to it but you have surpassed all my expectations. Keep up the good work. I know how it's easy to lose momentum for these things, as time passes.'

Joan, who had now turned a rather cute and flattering shade of pink, denied vehemently that this was going to happen to her. 'Thank you so much. I'm glad you're pleased. I really enjoyed writing it and I've plenty more ideas.'

'Excellent,' barked Elliot, never one to loiter over an agenda item when there was no need. 'When the next one's ready, run it past me first please, just like last time.'

'Of course.'

'Moving on. We're nearly done.' Rustling noises began as those at the meeting anticipated a fast approaching finish. Any other business?'

Elliott started piling up his papers in a manner guaranteed to dissuade most people from speaking.

'Yes, there is one thing,' John started. 'Something my partners asked me to bring up.'

Elliott looked at him with a hint of annoyance. Normally, matters for the meetings were discussed with him first as the vast majority he could deal with, negating the need for further discussion. It was so much simpler to present a fait accompli to his workforce and be spared the round-the-houses discussions that only ended up where they'd started.

Sensing his displeasure, John apologised. 'Sorry, Elliot, this only came up today and there was no time to mention it to you. You know the day we've all had.'

Elliot nodded sympathetically.

John took another sip of tea. 'The doctors are in total agreement that we have a splendid bunch of receptionists who look after us extremely well. But you will all have noticed how pressures of work have increased. You have an inkling of how much more we're expected to cram into already tight appointment times and you experience firsthand how demanding some characters can be. There is definitely the potential for mistakes to be made and of course we want to minimise that at all costs. In this litigious age, we can't be too careful. We must have robust systems in place.

'Sometimes messages are passed on in duplicate and sadly, last week, one message got missed altogether and was not passed on at all, which resulted in an urgent hospital appointment going to waste and a very disgruntled patient. Fortunately no harm was done. We have to decide on a system, either writing messages on paper, or emailing them. One or the other, preferably the email, then there is always a record. Pieces of paper have a habit of getting lost or thrown away. But definitely not both. Another thing that I and all the other partners find particularly hard is when we are interrupted by telephone calls while we're consulting. More than likely we are at an important, if not vital, part of the consultation or mid-examination. We have to ask the patient to wait outside, the call can take a while and it frequently generates more work so we wanted to lay down a few ground rules, come up with a better way of doing things.

'What I'd like to suggest it that we have a nominated receptionist for a partner. For example, Joan could be mine. She would be responsible for all of my messages and telephone calls. We're sure that this would decrease the likelihood of work being missed and be a much more efficient way of working. We appreciate that this may make slightly more work for you, as receptionists, but not a lot and in the long run, it will be an improvement all round.'

'I wish you'd discussed this with me first, John,' grumbled Elliott, who never liked being left out of the loop and also liked to present new plans as being his.

'We only came up with the thought at lunchtime and didn't want to leave it until the next meeting. I think it's a really good proposal, don't you?'

Elliott mumbled his agreement disgruntedly. 'I suppose so. I'd have liked to have some input though and then discuss it with Joan before telling everyone.'

John raised his hands in surrender. 'You're right, my mistake. It won't happen again.'

Elliott rolled his eyes in disbelief. 'I expect it will but never mind, we're talking about it now, so let's see what everyone thinks. Joan?'

She assumed a thoughtful stance. 'It might just work. On the face of it, it would be a far less messy system than what we do now. At least we receptionists would all know to whom we were accountable.'

Gary, Gemma and Elizabeth nodded, slowly, not sure that in fact more work was going to be created.

Joan cast a quick glance. 'How about we try it for a while? Say three months? And then discuss again.'

Elliott and John looked at each other. It was rare that a decision was made so rapidly at these meetings.

'Okay, then. Shall we move on, then?' Elliott scribbled some notes.

'Sorry to interrupt,' apologised Joan, 'but may I suggest the following pairings. Gary – you can be responsible for Dr Jennings and Dr Faber, Elizabeth, you can look after Dr Bonnington and any locums, Gemma will look after Dr Diamond and his registrar and I will look after Dr Britton, as he has requested.'

'How come you only have one doctor?' complained Gary.

Joan shot him an evil look. 'Because...he is senior partner and so inevitably will have more messages, more phone calls, more demand

and needs someone of vast experience to filter everything for him.'

'Well, I still think it's unfair,' grumbled Gary.

'It's been decided,' Joan told him. 'It's only a trial. Go into it with an open mind, for once. Change is important.'

'Hmm, it's all bloody change at this place. Leave your seat for too long and someone'll have taken it,' Gary had resorted to whispering to a sympathetic Elizabeth.

Amid the disgruntled grumblings, only one of the receptionists was walking on air as they went their separate ways. He had applauded her newsletter in front of the whole group. He had chosen her to be his right hand woman, not one of the others. He had asked for her by name. The conclusion was obvious – he wanted a reason for them to spend more time with each other and had constructed this plan especially.

Chapter Nine

'And may I enquire as to the nature of your call to Dr Britton?'

Joan was really getting into the swing of the new regime a week later.

Civility at all times. Joan was on a roll. How she loved wielding her recently awarded authority. Her body language spoke volumes as she sat up straighter in her chair whenever a call was passed on for her to deal with. She rounded her vowels and attached a slightly haughty, almost admonishing tone to her voice. This was so much easier than talking to people face to face. Not that she wasn't good at that too but no, with this new responsibility, she felt she had really found her niche. Rarely did anyone argue with her and it was such a refreshing change from home where most of her words were either contradicted or simply ignored.

'Now speak slowly and tell me again. Have I got this right? You're doing a sponsored bungee jump and you want a medical before you do it, to ensure nothing happens to you? Hmm. I'll get the duty doctor, who today happens to be Dr Britton, to ring you to discuss it. He should return the call this afternoon. Pardon? No, I can't be more precise than that...he's a busy man with a lot of other jobs to attend to, the majority of which are far more important than your request.'

She finished the call. 'Some people are clueless,' she said out loud but not to anyone in particular. 'How stupid can you be? Wanting to throw yourself over the side of a cliff wearing a rubber band and expecting a doctor to guarantee you won't hurt yourself. Ridiculous. Why isn't anyone prepared to take any responsibility for their own actions?'

The others all looked at her simultaneously, mouths slightly agape as she ranted. Whilst they felt that Joan had got the easy option with only one doctor to look after, they had never heard her talk quite like that to a patient before.

'You're really good at this, Joan,' cajoled Gary, Elizabeth murmuring her agreement.

Joan purred somewhat, smoothing down the front of her blouse and checking the collar where she had affixed a small but eye-catching brooch, hoping that this would look like a badge of office and different to her colleagues. It was inexpensive, like nearly all her jewellery, but the centre stone had a rather lustrous purple colour that caught the light attractively and complemented the blue of her uniform.

'Thank you, Gary,' she acknowledged, with a rare, brief approximation of a smile. 'I hope to lead by example.'

'Yes, you've got the exact right approach,' concurred Elizabeth, adjusting her headset.

'I've always admired the way you deal with the public,' went on Gary, Elizabeth nodding her support. 'You're so much better than any of us.'

Gemma sniggered.

Joan shot Gary a sideways glance, suspicious that he was being facetious. His hair was spiked up with gel, despite her repeated recommendations that this was not a good look for work. She did have to concede on this occasion that at least it was a gingery blond and possibly natural. Over the months since he had started, he had turned up with more or less every colour from one end of the spectrum to the other and there had been no alternative than to take him to one side and have a few words. Lambdale as a town, let alone the medical centre, was not ready for such outrageous fashion. Scrutinising his face, she decided that his comment was meant genuinely and smiled encouragingly.

'It's not as difficult as it looks. Part of it is simply practice, which you will all learn with time. I have been here rather longer than all of you, so that must be to my advantage. However, I do believe that there is also an innate ability to communicate. Some of us have it, some of us are not so lucky. I will be doing my utmost to make sure that all of you are able to perform to the very best of your ability. Perhaps Elliott will let us attend a course on communication skills, if I ask him nicely.'

Elizabeth and Gemma shared a worried look, which Joan spotted.

'There's no need to look like that, Elizabeth. I'm not going to start passing on my skills for a week or so yet. Let's see how this new system works first. Now then, you're next for tea, aren't you? Right, off you go. Don't be late back and do not, on any account, nip outside for a cigarette. It does not look good for anyone to be seen standing outside the surgery puffing away as if their life depended on it. Gary, move onto the front desk please, Gemma to the prescriptions phone. Quickly now, there's a queue of patients building up.'

Fortunately timed, Joan's phone rang and Elizabeth made a quick getaway while she could, pulling an exasperated face at Gary and Gemma on her way out.

Duty doctor that afternoon was John. It was not his favourite part of the week, due to the entirely unpredictable nature of the task. Famine or feast. Heaven or Hell, usually the latter. Past experience had taught him to expect the worst. Foolishly when the concept of duty doctor was first created, it had seemed on paper that this was some valuable administration time for the doctors to catch up with their own work, perhaps do some research or prepare for their appraisals but the reality was that there was never time even to start on any of these things for, as soon as they did, the telephone would ring, there would be a knock on the door or the computer would ping signifying the arrival of a patient who had been booked in at the last minute.

The fact that it was early December did not help. Patients were starting to worry about Christmas and trying to ensure that their holiday season would be germ-free. Winter bugs were having a field day, causing coughs, sore throats and colds and despite Joan's timely article in the practice newsletter, written by Clare, on how to deal with these things yourself and not bother the doctor, there was still the usual barrage of requests for antibiotics because 'it always goes onto my chest', or 'I was ill last Christmas so I don't want anything to spoil it this year'.

When John returned from his home visits and plonked down in his chair, there was already a considerable list of tasks for him to perform. His preference was to start with a clean slate, so that he felt in control from the beginning, so he wasn't happy. He unwrapped the sandwich –ham salad – that he had bought on his way back from the last call and took a large bite, deciding that he needed nourishment before he started on the onslaught. He was hardly able to speak as Joan knocked and came in.

'Sorry to bother you, Dr Britton but here's the folder with the prescriptions that need signing as soon as possible and there's an insurance form which really needs filling in today if you can. The patient's been on the phone three times about it already and the secretary has promised him it will be done asap.'

John sighed and viciously opened a packet of crisps.

'You look like you need a cuppa. I'll bring you one to wash down that sandwich. And there's some cake in the staff room – it's Elizabeth's birthday, so I'll sneak you a piece of that too.'

'Thanks, Joan, you're a star. Don't know what I'd do without you.'

Pushing his lunch to one side, John turned to his screen and dialled the number of the first call, feeling the need to get started rather than take a break and eat his lunch first.

'Hello, is that Miss Scott? Hello, it's Dr Britton here. How can I help you?'

Yet another bout of acute tonsillitis. After much persuasion and pleading for funding, Miss Scott was on the waiting list for a tonsillectomy. Mid-twenties, she was getting attacks every couple of months, missing work and her boss had started to threaten her with talk of her job being in jeopardy. In her spare time, she sang with a small band, performing locally and hoping for that big break which would probably never come. John was full of sympathy. He had seen her when she had had her last flare-up, systemically unwell with fever and loss of appetite, swollen throat and ugly white exudates all over the offending part of her anatomy.

'It's just like last time,' she told him. 'I feel dreadful.'

'I'll leave you a script for some penicillin,' he told her. ''You'd better have two weeks. Remember all the usual advice as well – plenty of fluids, paracetamol and, of course, if you feel any worse or you're not getting better, come on in and we'll have a look at you.'

Croaky thanks came down the receiver as he ended the call. John stuffed his mouth full of crisps and hurriedly typed in a prescription, printed it off, wrote up notes of the discussion and moved onwards. Automaton-like he worked his way through the list, grinding his teeth grimly when new tasks appeared. At times it felt like it was one step forwards and two backwards. The potential bungee jumper was pacified, offered a general check but told emphatically that the overall responsibility was his, not his doctor's.

'Sorry I've been so long,' apologised Joan, returning with a large mug of tea and a plate holding what looked as though it might be carrot cake. 'I got held up by Mr Wottle who was trying to bring his dog in with him. He was arguing that humans can go to into the vet's surgery, so it ought to work the other way round. He really should know better.'

John laughed. 'Yes he should! You have to deal with all sorts! I don't know how we'd manage without you. Anyway, here are the signed urgent scripts and there's an extra one for Naomi Scott. She's got tonsillitis again so needs some penicillin. She's coming in to pick it up from us, rather than from the pharmacy. I'll just keep plodding on but you know where I am if you want me.'

'Of course. Don't worry, we won't bother you unless we absolutely have to. Oh, I have just added the Simpson twins to your list. They're both feverish and have been sick.'

One thing about being busy is that time passes quickly and before he knew it, John realised that there was only half an hour left until the telephones would stop ringing and the doors would be locked. He congratulated himself on having caught up with everything and leant back in his chair, pondering on the evening ahead.

'I'm sorry, Dr Britton...' Joan's head appeared.

'Come in, come in.' He was feeling beneficent with the end of the day in sight.

'I...well, I don't really know how to say this.'

'Just say it, Joan.'

'I think there's been a mistake with this prescription.'

'Which one is that?'

Joan swallowed hard. 'This one for Miss Scott. For her tonsillitis. I thought you said penicillin.'

'Well, I did, that's what she usually has.'

'I thought as much but this script is for something called penicillamine. Is that the same thing?'

'Good God, no. Let me see...' He snatched the piece of paper from her hand.

John was horrified and felt a wave of chilled adrenaline shock his heart. Joan was right. He had prescribed a powerful drug, sometimes used for certain types of arthritis, with a host of horrible side-effects and certainly no use for tonsillitis. He must have caught sight of the first three syllables on the computer and then clicked on the incorrect drug. The dangers of hurrying. Thank goodness Joan had noticed before the patient had come in. This was potentially a serious error, mercifully averted.

But it was so unlike him. He had never done anything like this before. He prided himself on the methodical way in which he checked his record keeping and his prescribing. Ed often laughed at him, calling him anal, but John knew there was no way he would ever be able to change.

He felt sick. No harm had been done but the thought of what might have been... Well, it didn't bear thinking about. Tiredness was not an excuse. Nor was lack of enthusiasm. Compared to some days he was doing fine. Yes, it had been busy, but then, when wasn't it busy? No, there was no explanation for this error, which made it all the worse.

For the small part of what remained of his working day John checked and double checked, not simply what he had to do but he went through things he had done earlier, paranoid that there would be other mistakes, as yet unnoticed. To his relief, he found none and felt marginally better, briefly.

Haunted overnight by the spectre of 'what might have been', John's discomfiture remained and was little improved the following morning. Even a long discussion with Faye, a good supper of slow-roasted lamb shanks accompanied by a glass or two of a very smooth red wine had failed to help and his sleep had been disturbed repeatedly by waking and reliving near-misses that he had had in the past. On his way into work, he stopped the car and went into the local newsagents – the only shop open at that time of day – and bought the best box of chocolates they had to offer.

With a carefully rehearsed speech of thanks, he presented these to a delighted Joan after morning surgery and went off to the common room to share his indiscretion with his partners, knowing that this confession would be good for his soul.

Chapter Ten

Ivy was having a nightmare with Simeon while Joan was receiving her thank-you gift. He had come down that morning, after Joan had left, still in his pyjamas, slumped at the table and pushed away his bacon sandwiches. One round was never enough, Ivy always made him two. He was growing after all.

'I don't feel well, Granny,' he had announced, rather dramatically, laying his head on his folded arms and emitting a huge groan.

'Whatever's wrong?' Ivy was instantly alarmed. She almost dropped her cup of tea.

'My head hurts and I've got a sore throat and earache and tummy ache.'

There was a histrionic cough.

'Oh my goodness! You poor boy! Maybe you'll feel better if you eat...'

'No, I can't face food.'

'Then I think I'd better call your mother,' Ivy had decided.

'No!' had come Simeon's rapid and emphatic reply. 'Don't you remember – she said she was having problems with her phone.'

Ivy thought for a moment. 'No, I don't remember that. Anyway, I'll just call her at work.'

'Er, I'll be fine. Don't worry her, Granny, please.'

It had quickly been established that school was a non-starter. Ivy, having decided that he did indeed look rather flushed and felt hot to touch, hadn't wanted to take any chances. She had seen on television and read in magazines about meningitis, appendicitis and various other conditions ending with -itis and while she was unable to remember which symptoms applied to which diagnosis, she felt that the best way to monitor the situation was to have him with her. Joan sometimes came home with the most dreadful stories from work. People who were mildly unwell one minute and knocking on death's door the next.

Simeon, at that point, had agreed with her suggestion that maybe bed was the best place for him. Ivy had watched him trudge out of the room and promised she would be up to see him shortly with some paracetamol and a warm hot-water bottle. It had only been when she'd turned back to start clearing the table that she noticed that the bacon sandwiches had mysteriously disappeared and wondered if she had eaten them herself without thinking.

Secretly, Ivy was glad of the company. She found the part of the day when Simeon was at school difficult. Given the choice, she would have him home every day, mischievous as he was. Lonely and increasingly afraid, she had the habit of locking all the doors and not answering the phone unless she was sure it was Joan, who always gave a special three rings, rang off and then rang back again. Though she hated to admit it, Ivy lost track of time so easily these days that she had the television on constantly. Anyway, the noise of chat or music made her feel there was another presence in the house, which was reassuring. One day off would do him no harm. It was nearly the end of term, so she expected that little serious learning was taking place. Anyway, she knew he was a bright lad, very bright, gifted in many ways and probably bored and not pushed enough.

By mid-morning, however, she was beginning to wonder if she had made the right decision. Simeon looked a lot better, though flatly denied that he felt any different when asked and was now firmly established in front of the television, snuggled under his duvet and playing an ear-splitting game about zombies which was driving her mad. Any hopes she might have had about watching that entertaining programme about swapping houses were now extinct. Remarkably, his appetite had returned and when she suggested a small bowl of tomato soup for lunch, he had persuaded her to do chicken nuggets, chips and beans instead.

'Is there any cake, Granny?' he asked, as he wiped his plate clean, with a slice of white bread, thick with butter. 'I think I could manage a small bit.'

Ivy giggled. 'Well, you've certainly improved, I'm glad to say. As for cake, I don't think there is. There are some plain biscuits...'

'Ugh.'

'Well, it is the day your mum shops before she comes home, so we've pretty well run out of everything. Sure you won't have a biscuit?'

'Yuk. Haven't you any chocolate in your bag? You usually have.'

'And how would you know? Have you been peeping in my bag?'

Simeon shook his head, fingers crossed under the duvet, while Ivy trawled through the contents of her overlarge handbag, pushing aside a pair of slippers, a moth-eaten glove and an umbrella to plumb the depths completely. Just a boiled sweet covered with dust and fluff – no use to anybody, not even her grandson.

'Sorry, I've nothing. You'll just have to wait.'

At no pains to disguise his displeasure, Simeon kicked out under his duvet, grumbling and uttering some words which he definitely would not have used if his mother had been present. An idea came to him.

'Let's go and get some, Granny.'

'Now how can we do that? You're ill and I can't go and leave you on your own. Anyway, I've no money.'

'But you've got your card, so we can get some money, then buy some cake and come home. I think I need some fresh air and if I'm with you, neither of us will have to worry about anything.'

'Simeon, you are naughty! You're supposed to be ill, not eating cake.'

'I was ill this morning. Now I feel much better. It'd be a lovely surprise for Mummy when she comes home.'

Had she been present, wild horses would not have induced Simeon to refer thus to his mother. Occasionally, on a good day, it was 'mum'; more often it was another three-letter word, pertaining to a certain farm animal and producer of milk. However, it was one of his many tried and tested ways of getting round his grandmother.

As expected she began to prevaricate. 'Well,' she glanced in the direction of the window. 'It is fine and the sun's shining but you'd have to wrap up very warm as it's very chilly. I can't take the risk of you getting any worse and it going on your chest. You were a very wheezy baby and there was talk of asthma.'

'We can walk quickly and keep warm, Granny. It'll be lovely to go out together.'

His wheedling was slowly breaking down her defences.

'If you promise not to dawdle...'

'I do, Granny...'

'And we're not to be out above half an hour...'

'No, of course not...'

'And as soon as we're back, you're to have a hot drink and get back under that duvet..'

'Oh, yes, Granny.' He nodded in complete agreement. 'With a piece of cake.'

She studied his face and capitulated completely. 'Go on then. You'll get me shot! Get your coat. And scarf and hat and gloves please. I don't know what your mum'll have to say about this.'

'She'll not mind,' he called disappearing from the room at a gallop, 'and if we eat all the cake, there's no need to tell her!'

Credit where it's due, Simeon attired himself as requested in a large duffel coat with many pockets and a selection of his grandmother's knitting – hat, scarf and gloves, the latter attached to a long piece of elastic that went up one of his sleeves and down the other. If he had any gripes about it then he was polite enough not to let Ivy know. They walked side by side down the road, an odd couple to say the least, one calculating her every step, one bouncing up and down and sideways, prodding her and pointing out in all directions, which Ivy told him to stop as she said it made her feel dizzy. She had to make him slow down as well. Trying to maintain the same speed as him, chat and look at what he was showing her made her breathless and she was experiencing some unpleasant twinges behind her sternum, which she chose to ignore. At the cash point, Ivy took a couple of minutes to recover her breath before searching for her purse and pulling out her card. She still felt quite worn out and reached out for him.

'I need to sit down for a moment, Simeon. We've walked so quickly, I'm feeling woozy and need to use my angina spray.'

She made her way to a conveniently nearby bench and sat down inelegantly. Simeon snatched her debit card from her hand.

'Let me do it, Granny? Please? You sit there.'

'That would be a help. Look, get £20 out. That'll be more than enough and I'll have some left over to last me the rest of the week. I've spent enough on you this Christmas, though don't you go trying to find out what I've bought! Come here and I'll whisper the magic number that you need and don't tell anyone.'

'Of course not! As if I would.'

PIN disclosed, Ivy took a deep breath, took a squirt of her spray under her tongue and closed her eyes. She was feeling a little better but not looking forward to the walk home. As she wondered about how much a taxi might cost, for there was no suitable bus they could catch, Simeon, with his back to her, carefully entered her details, which he had committed to memory for future reference, requested £50, surreptitiously pocketed £30 and then dutifully returned the card with two crisp ten-pound notes. As he anticipated, Ivy opted to stay where she was, rather than face the supermarket with him. Armed with one of the notes, he ran into the shop, chose a large, party-sized chocolate cake and a slab of angel cake and paid for these along with a goodly selection of sweets and chocolates. The latter he then stuffed in his coat pockets before bouncing out to find his grandmother.

'All done! Let's go home and start eating!'

Somehow Ivy managed the walk home, even if it did take her twice as long and involved numerous stops to view people's gardens, a process which infuriated her grandson. By the time they got home though, his desire for sticky, sweet cake trumped his fractiousness and he nobly volunteered to make a cup of tea while Ivy took her coat off and sat down. She promptly fell asleep, chin on her chest, snoring stertorously. Simeon looked at her, not without some affection, before taking the entire chocolate cake up to his room to eat while he listened to the sort of music his mother would refer to as noise.

Later that evening, Joan found the angel cake and asked where it had come from.

Ivy did her best to explain, hoping that Joan wouldn't be angry. She wasn't. In truth, she was far too elated by her gift of chocolates to try to sort out another example of Simeon taking advantage of his Granny.

'I thought we bought a chocolate cake as well,' Ivy mused, opening the cupboard door, where all she found was a pint of milk that she had put there earlier, rather than in the fridge.

'No, we didn't,' Simeon was quick to correct her. 'Don't you remember, Granny? We were going to buy chocolate cake but then we changed our minds because angel cake is one of your favourites and I said that because you'd been kind enough to take me out, you should choose what sort of cake we bought?'

Ivy was puzzled. She must have made a mistake. How silly of her. She smiled and ruffled her beloved grandson's hair. 'Such a good boy, always thinking of others.'

'Never mind,' added Joan, 'Dr Britton gave me some chocolates today – a personal gift! Let's have those. They're in such a lovely box, I think I'll keep it.'

Chapter Eleven

Christmas was on the doorstep and the weather was damp, depressing and unseasonably mild. Around the market square hung sad-looking droopy decorations, doing their best to instil festive spirit into shoppers comprising of locals and the occasional day tripper. The Victorian market was a washout. Held annually, two weeks before Christmas, the stall-holders dressed in Dickensian outfits and roast chestnuts were on sale along with anachronistic kebabs and hot pulled-pork sandwiches with apple sauce. Delicious rose to the occasion and provided the best mince pies (warm of course, with cream if desired), turkey baps with cranberry sauce or oatmeal stuffing (or both) and savoury or sweet vegetarian pasties full of Christmas spices. It was usually hugely popular but the torrential rain was a deterrent to even the most intrepid visitors; mob caps and topcoats failed to have the same impact when covered with hooded anoraks and all was packed away by shortly before lunchtime.

'We need some frost! Some really cold weather so that it feels like Christmas,' declared Ellie one day, standing at the window of the common room watching the rain batter against the glass. 'This is so dreary. You should see the mud at the paddock gate. Poor Smudge and Jester are up to their knees in it. They just stand there, waiting to come into their stable. Can't say I blame them though. I'd probably do the same if I was a pony.'

'We all need a break,' Ed replied grimly, handing Ellie an envelope. 'I think this has been one of the worst runs up to Christmas that I've ever worked. Here, Mrs Tonbridge left this for you. She came to see me today, wanting me to sort out her back pain that she's had for thirty-five years in time for her cousin coming to take her out for a turkey lunch.'

Ellie rolled her eyes. 'Poor you, but that's kind of her, a card! She's never sent me one before. Oh no, it's not! It's a list of what prescriptions she needs before the holiday! Typical!'

But at least it made them laugh, albeit briefly.

The medical centre was stretched to its capacity. It was the same every year, patients clamouring to be seen until Christmas Eve, when suddenly, round about lunchtime, it went deathly quiet, as if someone had unplugged the phone lines, leaving the building feeling eerily silent but at least allowing most of the staff to go home early. Around three in the afternoon, Joan would produce a bottle of sherry and each of the receptionists was allowed a glass to celebrate, a small one mind you.

Clare had a humdinger of a cold with a hacking cough. All things considered, she ought to have been at home in bed. The others had told her to take a day off, stay indoors, imbibe hot drinks and paracetamol but she had refused, knowing too well what chaos that would result in for her colleagues left behind with their own work and a share of hers as well. She looked terrible; rather like Rudolf she was red nosed but the remainder of her face was pasty coloured. Ellie noticed that over a polo-necked jumper, Clare had on two cardigans yet still sat hugging herself and shivering. Her cough made the patients cower and the window fittings rattle, such was its ferocity and one or two even acknowledged that she was in a far worse state than they were.

'I've had one cold after another since Tom started with the child-minder,' she snuffled, miserably, ripping open a sachet of flu remedy and pouring the contents into a mug of hot water and stirring. 'He gets them too but seems to bounce back much quicker than I do and David never gets anything.'

'We've only a couple of days to go now,' Ellie commented, 'then we're closed for four whole days, so that'll really give you a chance to get better.'

'It's the first Christmas that Tom will realise what's going on though. I wanted so much for us all to have a proper family day but I'm hardly going to be much fun like this. David's only got two days off as he's on call at the weekend and he's bound to be busy as it's such a bad and lonely time for some people. '

'Funny, isn't it?' agreed Ellie. 'If you were to believe adverts on TV, you'd think that everyone is overwhelmingly happy, stuffing themselves with food and having wonderful family times, where as in reality, families are at each other's throats by mid afternoon and those on their own are desperate.'

'Don't be so pessimistic, Ellie!' called Ed, from the kitchen area, where he was cutting a large piece of cake brought in as a thank-you from a patient.

'Sorry,' Ellie replied. 'It's this rain, it's so depressing. Cut me a piece too would you – it looks really good. Who made it?'

'That patient of John's – the one with recently diagnosed rheumatoid.'

As though he had heard his name, the door opened and John came in, carrying two bottles of whisky and one of wine.

'I quite like this job, after all,' he announced, to the others' amusement.

Aware of a stern glance coming from Ellie's direction, John studiously avoided the cake and made himself a coffee.

'Some patients are so kind,' he commented. 'Often the ones who can least afford it.'

Clare sneezed violently, splinting one side of her chest with her hand. 'Ouch, that hurt!'

'Why don't you go home?' Ellie suggested, gently. 'We can manage here. Honestly. You've done morning surgery and we'll soon divide the visits up between us – there aren't that many – and we can juggle things round this afternoon. And before you even begin to speak, no, you are not letting anybody down.'

Clare looked from one to another of them, pathetically. 'Well, I could do with some sleep, it's true. I could catch a few hours while Tom's at the childminder. David's picking him up today...'

'Then go! Take care of yourself for once. We're fine, aren't we?'

They all nodded in agreement.

For once, Clare didn't need asking twice. As Ellie commented afterwards, she must have been feeling awful as she gave in without an argument. She made her way down to her consulting room for her bag and coat, quickly leaving a message for David to let him know what was happening.

Stopping at the reception desk, she spoke to Joan. 'I'm so sorry, I've got to go home. I feel terrible.'

'I'm afraid to say that you look it, Dr Jennings. You get off now.' Joan was full of sympathy. 'Oh, just before you go...'

Clare turned. 'Yes?'

'One of the patients, I forget which one – I've seen so many of them this morning,' Joan laughed, 'was asking what Dr Britton liked in the way of food and drink. He wants to bring him in a gift, I think. I really had no idea at all, so promised to ring him back. I thought you might be able to help but obviously, don't tell him!'

Clare smiled, wanly. 'No, of course I won't. Well,' she paused for a moment, 'he likes malt whisky, a good red wine, loves blue cheese. Is that any help?'

'Oh, perfect thank you. I'll call that patient right away before I forget, which I might well do once the afternoon gets into top gear.'

'I'm off home then. Hopefully I'll see you tomorrow.'

'Only if you are considerably better,' Joan warned her. 'No one's indispensable.' And while she spoke, she was feeling the two fifty-pound notes that had arrived that morning with a rather ostentatious card – from Greg. Plus contact details of all things. Well, she wasn't going to need those. The card would be consigned to the bin once she got home, but the money – she wasn't going to throw that away. Oh no, she had a much better use for it.

Chapter Twelve

The carpet was invisible, covered with torn and crumpled wrapping paper, Cellophane and ripped boxes. Simeon was not one to open his presents either slowly or carefully and Joan had abandoned long ago any attempt to keep things tidy. Well, it was Christmas Day, she supposed.

In the corner of the room, on the table, with everything else that had simply been pushed to one side, was the same tree that came out every year, rescued from some dim recess of the loft where it had been shoved eleven months previously. Looking rather the worse for wear, with a tipsy tilt to the left, tired baubles hung down between the strands of tinsel which had been thrown on hastily rather than tastefully arranged. Several of the tiny light bulbs had long given up the ghost so the twinkling was patchy at best. They were to be confined to the bin in the New Year, Joan had already decided.

Ivy was nodding, chin on chest, schooner of sherry, her second, a bit like the Christmas tree, at a dangerous angle in her lap. The exertions of the morning and the ridiculously early start had proved too much for her and she was now oblivious to the cacophony of noise around her – the television, the new computer game, the sound of lunch being prepared. A pink paper crown sat on her head, falling over one eye, Simeon having insisted on having crackers with breakfast, so they could all wear their hats all day.

Joan, like many others before her, was wondering why on earth she spent so long preparing Christmas dinner for the three of them when it was eaten in seconds. It didn't seem fair, yet how nice it could be, sitting around the table all three of them, taking their time, chatting and laughing, having a rest between courses. A laughable dream, she thought, almost blown back by the heat of the oven as she opened the door to check on the potatoes. Not the tidiest of cooks, what little work surface she had was occupied by pans or dishes because, as usual, she was tailor-making the meal to suit everyone's individual tastes. No stuffing for Simeon, who wanted bacon wrapped round sausages, mash for Ivy who struggled with the crispy roast potatoes. Mercifully only trifle for dessert, but even that had meant making an alcohol-free version for Simeon, who was giving new meaning to the expression hyperactive and did not need any encouragement.

Joan's hair was a victim of the hot atmosphere and she knew it. Strands kept falling forwards and having to be pushed back behind her ears and now there was little resemblance to the style she had tried to create when she got up. Her cheeks were scarlet and she could feel sweat trickling down under the collar of her best dress, which only came out for high days and holidays. Why did she bother, she repeatedly asked herself, knowing full well that if she didn't, then it simply wouldn't feel right.

She smiled, hearing Simeon shriek happily. At least his presents seemed to be a success. He had provided the obligatory list beforehand and despite many of the items being way out of her price range, she had managed to get quite a lot of things for him that he wanted and Ivy had come up trumps with some extra cash, so between them he had done quite well out of them.

She was on the home run. She was juggling gravy-making with doing the vegetables and warming the plates. There was no way that the table in the lounge could be cleared enough for them to sit down, which was a shame as to eat in there would have been much more special so the kitchen table would have to do. It would be cramped and just like any other meal that they didn't eat off trays on their laps but never mind. There was a red tablecloth with snowflakes on it and paper napkins to match.

Carefully, she arranged glacé cherries on the top of some fanned-out melon slices which were to be their starter. It looked very pretty, she thought, as she placed them on the table and called Ivy and Simeon to say that the meal was ready. She wasn't particularly surprised when there was no response. Not many would have been able to make themselves heard over that row. Picking up wrapping-paper bits as she walked into the lounge, she nudged her mother gently and caught the glass before its contents went all over the cushions. Ivy came to with a start, momentarily completely confused as to where she, what was happening and why on earth she had a paper crown falling off her head. Simeon laughed unkindly but thundered into the kitchen, roaring at the top of his voice, leaving the television still on. Helping her mother to her feet, Joan turned the sound to mute and relished the sudden, momentary absence of any noise.

'I think I need the bathroom, dear,' Ivy rather spoiled things by saying. 'And a change of underwear.'

By the time Ivy was clean and dry and she and Joan sat down at the table, Simeon had of course eaten his melon and started on a box of biscuits, too impatient to wait. Deftly, Joan whisked them away and he sat grumpily while the two women delicately ate their melon slivers, clearly, to his mind, trying to take as long as possible just to be awkward.

The main course was a success, more or less. Simeon whined for chips and tomato ketchup but Joan stood firm. Healthy portions were dealt out and consumed, apart from Ivy who, still woozy from the sherry, stuck to mashed potato and gravy with a few carrots. Joan made several attempts at conversation but her fellow diners were not obliging and she gave up, instead enjoying her cooking as best she could and not thinking about the washing up, a job that would surely fall her way, there being no volunteers to help.

'There's a good film on later, I thought we could watch together. A comedy – you know, one of those ones with really clever animals in...' Joan made a move to clear the plates.

'Yuk!' replied Simeon, 'there's a horror film on the other channel. I saw a bit of it this morning. It looked really good, lots of blood!'

Ivy looked suitably shocked. 'I don't think we want anything like that on Christmas Day, dear. Let's try the one your mum's suggesting. You can cuddle up with me on the sofa and we'll perhaps find a tiny box of chocolates that we can dip into as we watch.'

The plates were cleared and added to the untidy pile of pots and pans by the sink. Dollops of trifle had flopped into the best glass bowls and been handed round. About to take her first mouthful and noticing that Simeon was trying to distract his grandmother so that he could swap her bowl for his, Joan chastised him with a gentle slap on the hand, precipitating a wave of crocodile tears and bad temper. He deliberately spilt custard on the table, threw his spoon down with a vehemence that made the table shudder and without asking for permission, he stormed out of the room, slamming the door behind him for maximum effect. Within seconds, the television could be heard blaring out again.

Ivy and Joan sighed in unison and toyed with what was left in their bowls. Joan felt that the meal was not only over, but ruined.

'What that boy needs,' stated Ivy, stifling a hiccup, 'is a father. Someone to look up to.'

The deterioration continued as the afternoon progressed. Not only did Simeon become increasingly hard to tolerate as he insisted on certain programmes and complained bitterly if denied but he continued to gobble chocolates and nuts the whole time. Joan's suggestion of a nice walk before it got dark was met with derision from her son and an apology from her mother who felt too tired to go, so she went alone, was only gone for perhaps thirty minutes and returned to tackle the washing up. At least her head felt the benefit of some fresh air. It had started to throb horribly half way through lunch and painkillers had had no effect at all.

In the kitchen she noticed with sadness that the sherry trifle bowl was now empty and she didn't need to spend much time realising who

65

the culprit was. Thank goodness it was only one day a year and if only the same could be said for her son's dreadful behaviour. Not keen on rejoining her family in the lounge, Joan slowly worked her way through the dishes, doing a thorough job, as always, but then drying everything, putting everything neatly away, stacking up the leftovers in the fridge and wiping down all the surfaces, by which time the only evidence that Christmas dinner had occurred was the lingering smell of roast turkey.

She brewed two cups of tea, looking forward to a sit down and putting her feet up for a good while. Surely nobody would want more than a bit of a sandwich, if that, in what was left of the day. Ivy was asleep, again. Simeon was lying on the sofa, devouring the contents of a tin of chocolates, picking out all his favourites, throwing the wrappers on the floor. Finally comfortable, Joan wondered if other people's Christmas Days were as disastrous as theirs. What would Dr Britton be doing? I bet they have their dinner in the evening, she thought, on a beautifully decorated table, the sort of thing you see in glossy magazines, all silver and red, shimmering in candlelight. Would all his family be there? Maybe. If they were they'd all be behaving politely and with decorum. No way would they be arguing and refusing to eat Brussels sprouts. Most importantly, I wonder if he's enjoying the cheese and wine that I sent him.

Simeon sat up suddenly, announced that he didn't feel very well, went green and vomited into the tin. The contents of Joan's stomach churned empathically but the rest of her felt annoyed.

'You've eaten too much today,' she scolded him. 'No wonder this has happened. Now get up to bed and have a lie down and I'll be up in a minute to see how you are.'

He must have felt bad, she thought, as he left with barely a murmur of protest. His footsteps thumped up the stairs, increasing in speed and then there were further unpleasant noises to be heard in the bathroom. Shaking her head, Joan followed him.

Surprisingly, her evening turned out to be really quite pleasant.

With one dependent sleeping in his bed and the other declaring she needed an early night, the excitement having proved too much for Ivy, Joan was left on her own, a turn of events that she was delighted with. She found an old but engaging detective film to watch, poured a glass of wine to have with a cold turkey sandwich and snuggled down in her chair, feet cosy in the slippers that Ivy had given her, ready to enjoy what was left of the day and happy with her own secret thoughts.

Chapter Thirteen

All was not well the next morning but this time it was Ivy who was the cause for concern. Joan had woken on numerous occasions during the night to hear the raucous flush of the toilet and the sound of her mother padding back to the bedroom. Then to make matters worse, there was incontrovertible evidence of Ivy having wet the bed at some other point, soaking not only the sheets but the mattress and duvet cover as well. Ivy looked pale and unwell when she arrived at the breakfast table, still in her nightdress, which incidentally was inside out, and with her hair sticking up all over the place, much to Simeon's amusement. She turned down the offer of any food and put six teaspoonfuls of sugar in her cup of tea before complaining that it was too sweet.

'Not going to work, dear?' she asked Joan, who was buttering toast for Simeon.

'Mum, it's Boxing Day,' was the reply.

'Is it really? Well, I think I might have a stroll down to the shops this morning.'

'They'll all be closed. It's a holiday. We can still have a nice walk though, if you'd like.'

'Oh, I don't think so, if the shops are shut. We can't buy anything, can we? Whatever will we eat today? I can't have Simeon going hungry...'

'We've plenty of food. Don't worry. The fridge is groaning because there's so much stuff in there. I'm going to do you some nice turkey in gravy for your dinner.'

Ivy looked worried. 'I don't know if I'll manage that, dear. Maybe after I've been to the shops, I'll feel more like it. Have a bit of an appetite.'

Joan looked at her. The more they chatted, the more obvious it became that Ivy was very muddled, considerably more than usual. She had no idea, not only what day it was, but also where she was and the situation was not helped by Simeon who took some evil delight in telling her they were in different places, such as the hospital, a hotel and on another planet, thus baffling her further. The final straw, as far as Joan was concerned, was when Ivy asked where her mother was.

'I think you need to go back to bed, Mother,' decided Joan. 'You need some rest. Have a really quiet day. We're all tired out after yesterday. It's always the same. There's such a build up to Christmas and then everything falls flat.'

Ivy got up from her chair, filled a pan with milk and put it on the cooker hob.

'What are you doing now?' asked Joan.

'Making a hot water bottle, of course,' she replied indignantly. 'To take back to bed with me as that's where you've insisted I go.'

Simeon sniggered into his toast. 'Granny's lost the plot!'

Gently removing the pan from her mother's hands, Joan steered her patient back upstairs and helped her into bed. Her balance was not good at all and there was one very hairy moment half way when Joan was fearful that Ivy might fall, taking her with her.

Ivy relaxed back into the pillows with relief. 'That feels nice, dear. Thank you. I do feel I might be sick, though. Can I have a bucket please?'

Joan was baffled. What on earth was going on? Had Ivy and Simeon caught some sort of bug? Was it something they'd eaten? Heaven forbid that it was her cooking. Everything had been piping hot, including the turkey which any gourmet would have pronounced dry and overdone. Why was Ivy so confused all of a sudden? And most importantly, what on earth was she supposed to do about it on Boxing Day?

There was of course the out-of-hours GP service but she had heard the doctors at the surgery being so derogative about time wasters, she was reluctant to go down this route. Today though was Friday and the weekend loomed large as a hurdle to be surmounted before normal surgeries resumed and at that point the doctors would be overwhelmed by those who had hung on until after the holidays. No suitable solution sprung to mind. She would simply have to see how things went for the next day and, if all else failed, ring for some help.

Despite Joan's best efforts, Ivy continued to deteriorate and Joan felt shattered after a day and night of repeated sheet changing, circuitous conversations which made no sense and no sleep. On the Saturday morning, in desperation, it suddenly occurred to her that she could go and ask for some advice at the pharmacy. Alan Gough was an obliging man, who would surely tell her what it was best for her to do. If he said to ring the out-of-hours services then that would be fine, because she would be able to say to them that she'd been told to ring by a professional.

Leaving Simeon in charge and telling him on no account to let Ivy get out of bed and that she would be back within fifteen minutes, Joan drove the short distance to the market square and gratefully saw that the pharmacy was open. Waiting in the queue, which was considerable as people sought remedies to settle their indigestion or hangovers, she felt a hand pat her on the shoulder and looked round to see, to her joy, John Britton, looking relaxed and off duty in a waxed jacket, dark blue woolly jumper (a Christmas present perhaps?) and some faded jeans.

'Hello, Joan,' he began. 'Had a nice Christmas?'

'Oh, Dr Britton! How lovely to see you. Yes, very pleasant, very quiet. How about you?'

'A bit crazy, definitely not quiet. Lots of fun. I needed to get out for a bit, so I pretended we'd run out of toothpaste. Don't tell anyone!'

Joan laughed with him, thrilled to be included in his secret. 'I know the feeling. There's only the three of us, but even then, it's still nice to have some time on your own.'

'So how's your mum keeping these days?' John asked.

Joan paused. Surely this was an opportunity not to be missed. 'Well, if I'm honest, I'm a bit worried about her.' She explained what had happened. 'I think I'll have to bring her in to see you next week, if you've an appointment free.'

John scratched his head. 'It sounds to me as though she needs to be seen today, not next week. It might be something simple like a urine infection and we could get her on some antibiotics and she'd pick up in no time.'

'I'd not thought of that,' admitted Joan. 'I've been so busy trying to keep things going...'

'Of course you have.'

'I'll go home and ring the out-of-hours service right away.'

John shook his head. 'They'll be run off their feet and you'll be waiting hours. I tell you what. Let me go home, get my bag and prescription pad and I'll come round myself in about thirty minutes. Would that suit you?'

'Oh, Dr Britton! That would be so wonderful. But it's your off-duty time. I'll never forgive myself for intruding into it. Your family need you.'

'Never mind them. I'll be back with them before they realise I've gone. I'll just pay for this,' he waved two tubes of toothpaste at a slightly harassed-looking Alan Gough, who nodded, put down the correct money on the counter, 'and I'll see you at yours, shortly. Just remind me of the address...'

No longer needing to consult with the pharmacist, Joan sped home, surveyed the mess with dismay and scurried around trying to recreate some level of order in record time. As the front door bell rang, there was an almighty thud upstairs and Simeon yelled, 'Granny's fallen over!'

John had never visited Joan's home before. She had always brought Ivy or Simeon to the surgery and their visits were infrequent. If he was taken aback by the chaotic appearance of the front garden, the broken flags and weed-ridden gravel that made up the path and the paint peeling off the front door, he said nothing but marched in cheerfully and strode up the stairs after Joan.

Ivy was lying on the floor, resembling a giant chrysalis as she was tangled up in a white sheet. Entering her bedroom was like stepping back in time. The walls were decorated in fading, flowery, old-fashioned wallpaper which contrasted sharply with the chintzy frills covering over the kidney-shaped dressing table, on which was an array of pink and blue curlers, Kirby grips and a brush full of silver hairs. On a stool nearby was a neat pile of laundry, waiting to be put away.

Kneeling down beside her, John immediately realised that Ivy was hopelessly confused. She was rambling incoherently and unable to answer even the simplest of questions. The asymmetry of her face made him wonder if she had had a stroke. He gently unravelled the sheet, which was sodden. The ammoniacal smell burned his nostrils. For sure, there was a urine infection going on and possibly all sorts of other problems.

'I'd rather not move her,' he explained, after he had finished the best examination he was able to perform in the circumstances. 'She seems in discomfort if she moves so I think the best thing is to get an ambulance and we'll get her to Accident and Emergency. She can be checked out thoroughly there. I'm sure they'll keep her in for at least a couple of days.'

'Oh no! Can't we wait and see how she is tomorrow?' Joan was horrified.

'Certainly not. She can't stay here on the floor for starters, can she?' He reached into his pocket for his mobile phone.

Simeon, who had been uncharacteristically quiet until now, jumped up and down excitedly. 'Wow, an ambulance! Coming here! Will it have sirens and lights?'

'Very possibly,' John looked at him, seeing a chubby lad with a sulky face, which included chocolate around his mouth. His recovery after a night's sleep had been rapid.

'Simeon, get Granny's case from the wardrobe, please,' Joan asked.

'No! Get it yourself. I don't want Granny to go to hospital.' He stamped his feet.

'She has to go and get better. We don't like her being ill, do we?'

'But she promised to take me to the pantomime next week. Everyone in my class is going. I can't be the only one who doesn't go.'

John turned to him. 'Well she can't take you while she's poorly, so the sooner she gets well, the better it is for all of us.'

Fortunately for all, the sound of sirens in the distance had Simeon running to the window to await the arrival of the ambulance. Joan hastily threw some spare nighties, a wash bag, towel and slippers into a battered vanity case and looked around hopelessly to see if she ought to add anything else.

'Don't worry,' John assured her. 'I'm sure Ivy'll be fine in a couple of days. Let's hope she's not broken any bones because if she hasn't she'll be home in no time. Are you going to go in the ambulance with her?'

'I'd not thought of that,' Joan was worried. 'This is all so difficult. I've Simeon to think of too. Perhaps we should both go with her.'

'Could Simeon stay with the neighbours? Or a friend?'

'Oh I couldn't possibly bother anyone on a holiday,' Joan replied hurriedly, not wishing to admit the real reason for her having nobody to look after her son. 'I think it's a better idea if Mother goes now and we can follow down later.'

'That's sensible. Ivy will have to have a number of tests and x-rays to start with, so probably best if you go down once she's on the ward and comfortable. You'd only be sitting around waiting and Simeon doesn't look like someone who takes kindly to being patient.'

'I'm afraid he's not.'

'They're here, they're here!' Simeon screeched at the top of his voice, making Ivy jump.

The house seemed suddenly quiet when Joan closed the door having watched the rear lights of the ambulance disappear down the road and round the corner. She felt rather nauseous and shivery, which she presumed was shock. Simeon, however, had returned to his favourite chair and video game. John was packing his stethoscope back into his bag and putting his jacket on.

'Thank you so much for coming.' Joan gushed. 'Can I get you a cup of tea? I think we need one. That's the least I can do to thank you.'

'You're very kind, Joan, but not on this occasion. I shall ring the hospital later to see how Ivy's doing and here's my home number for you to ring, if you need my help before Monday. Don't be afraid to use it. Anytime, day or night. Okay?'

He held his hand out and she grasped it in both of hers. Was it her imagination, or did he hold on to hers rather longer than someone would normally? And he had given her his number! And he had only turned down the offer of a cup of tea 'on this occasion' which implied that there would be another time!

Perhaps Christmas was turning out not to be so bad after all.

Chapter Fourteen

'I felt rather sorry for her, if I'm honest.'

It was the Sunday evening and John was having a lazy supper with Faye who had done wonders with the leftovers and conjured up a delicately spiced curry and served it with rice and salad, fresh, light flavours that were just the ticket after two days of excessive indulgence. He was not feeling his best, the black cloud having settled above his head round about mid-afternoon and increased ominously since, as the prospect of the following day back at work loomed ever nearer. Their family had all departed in different directions to various New Year celebrations and he felt an overwhelming urge to take down the Christmas tree and get the house back to normal. Not that he'd suggest it as he knew how Faye loved Christmas and New Year.

'Where did you say she lived?' Faye asked.

'On the council estate. Her house is rather dilapidated, to put it mildly. I've never really thought of what it might be like but I'm a bit horrified now I've found out.'

'You've mentioned her mother and that awful-sounding child. Isn't there a husband around?'

'No, I seem to remember her telling me ages ago that he'd disappeared off the scene. She's been coming to see me with chronic headaches – and I can't find a cause. She's always denied any social or psychological problems but this visit has given me a lot of insight. I'll have another word with her next week.'

Faye put a plate of cheeses and a bowl of grapes on the table. John paused over his choice, wondering if he might dare to ask if there was any chocolate mousse left over.

'I really have no idea who left this at the surgery. It must have cost a fortune. A hamper full of cheeses, pâtés and two bottles of excellent claret. But no card, so I can't even write and say thank you.'

'It came from that fabulous old-fashioned grocer's in Harrogate. You know the one I mean. I've seen hampers like this in their window. They cost about a hundred pounds! Someone's bound to mention it when they come in to see you. But to go back to Joan,' continued Faye, who had opted for the ripe Stilton without any hesitation, 'she must be managing on a shoestring. I mean, a receptionist's pay isn't particularly good, is it?'

John, mouth full, shook his head. 'No, it's rubbish really, considering all they're expected to do these days. As a practice, we pay the top of the scale but it's still not very much. Joan does the practice newsletter and Elliott told me that she'd been asking for a bonus for doing it. Now I know why.'

'From the ones you've brought home, she's doing a good job. The article on low-fat diets which she called "Flab-u-less to Fab-u-lous in 6 weeks" was excellent.'

'Ellie wrote it of course. Though admittedly Joan came up with the title.'

'But she wrote the one about you and that was very good. Though why it was so much longer than the ones she did on Clare and Ellie, I don't know, or why I didn't get a mention...'

'Ha ha – the privileges of being senior partner.' John laughed.

Faye was thinking. 'Perhaps she could get a job in the evening,' she suggested.

'She already has one. Looking after a mother who has advancing dementia and a son who is very difficult. Both of which by themselves are full-time jobs. I'm afraid that life is going to get harder for her as Ivy gets worse.'

Faye went to switch on the coffee machine and paused for a moment. 'I've just remembered. The tennis club want someone to computerise all their paperwork which is so disorganised it's not true. I'd sort of volunteered but I really don't want to and I'm sure they'd pay to have it done properly. It wouldn't be a lot of money but do you think Joan would be interested?'

John finished his mouthful and refilled his glass. 'Maybe. It's something she could do in an evening, from home, isn't it?'

'I don't see why not. Do you want me to ask her?'

'Thanks, yes that's good of you.'

John reflected on the weekend. He had enjoyed Christmas. The only downside was that it was always so hectic that it passed in a trice. It had been fabulous to see his family and the grandchildren. Now it would most likely be Easter before he saw them again. That was the problem of them leaving home to seek their fortunes. They ended up so far away. He must count his blessings though. At least they were all in this country.

Tomorrow promised to be terrible. A queue would be waiting at the door of the medical centre before it was opened and the phones would be red hot all day. The practice policy of not allowing any of the doctors to take holiday in the week between Christmas and New Year, though unpopular with some, was one of Elliot's best ideas. Definitely all hands were needed on deck, as it were, to cope with the demand. Then of course there was another Bank Holiday on New Year's Day and then another bad day after that, which in some ways was even worse as people no longer had anything to look forward to apart from the dark, gloomy days of January and February.

Next year, he was definitely going to finalise his retirement plans. It wasn't fair on the others to keep them in the dark. They knew he was on the verge of making a decision and, supportive as they were, it was only fair that he gave them as much warning as possible as they would then have to decide whether they were going to take on a replacement partner or not. Much as he loved parts of the job, he knew instinctively that it was time to bow out. Quit while he was ahead before feelings of resentment started to set in. A meeting with his accountant beckoned, some calculations, financial projections and, with any luck, he might just have worked his very last Christmas.

That was the first of his resolutions. He had decided on only two (which was two more than usual) and the other was to get to grips once and for all with his diabetes. Pretending that it wasn't there was no way to carry on. How appalled would he be if a patient behaved like that? No, he'd had time to digest what was going on and much as he might dislike it, it wasn't going to go away. From January 1st, he was going to be a reformed character, totally re-jig his diet, lose weight and start exercising. Unsure as to just how he was going to exercise, that was a decision yet to be made, but he'd taken the first step, as it were, by deciding to do it. He knew how relieved his decision would make Faye. Her tact on the subject was characteristic.

Another glass of wine poured and feeling rather satisfied with himself for his decisions, he helped Faye with the washing up, drying while she washed, ten minutes of rather lovely togetherness, not saying much but appreciating each other's presence. Faye instinctively knew how he was feeling. She witnessed this every weekend and had tried everything she could think of to make it better. She had tried making lovely dinners, taking him out for dinner, having friends round, going to friends, but nothing made any difference. As the clock ticked, John became more withdrawn and gloomy.

They spent the rest of the evening in the lounge, no lights on apart from those on the tree, which was romantically magical and the glare from the television which was intrusive but, for once, hidden away amongst all the predictable repeats, they found a rather good play which they both enjoyed.

Tomorrow will come and it will go as well, John reassured himself, over and over. If this is the effect the job is having on me, then it's time to bow out while I can still do it gracefully.

Chapter Fifteen

John thought that Joan looked shattered, emotionally and physically. Though she was dressed smartly as ever, her posture slumped and lacked its usual authoritative élan and the pallor of her face with big dark rings around her eyes gave away the fact that sleep had not been forthcoming.

He came back to the surgery at lunchtime and rather than sitting up in the common room, took his lunch – a sandwich, iced finger (well, it wasn't January 1st yet) and mince pie (well, it was still Christmas) and a cup of coffee – back down to his consulting room and asked her to join him. His morning had been as he expected, busy but, fortunately, a myriad of minor ailments rather than anything serious.

Joan flopped down into the patient's chair with a heavy sigh.

He smiled at her sympathetically. 'So, how are things? I wasn't expecting to see you at work.'

She pulled a face. 'Difficult, but improving. I must thank you so much once again for coming out on your day off. It was so very, very kind of you and such a help to me. I really hadn't known what to do.'

'Not a problem. I've rung the hospital today and it seems that it was a urine infection that discombobulated Ivy. But then they've probably explained all that to you anyway. Great news that she hadn't broken anything in that fall, though, wasn't it?'

'Oh, yes. She must have bounced! The hospital has been wonderful. They've said she should be home by the New Year, if all goes well. She's already complaining about the food, which has to be a good sign. And she's managing to walk up and down the ward with the help of one of those frames. Simeon's put some tinsel round it to cheer her up!'

'Well, she's in good hands. But what about you? How are you coping with everything? What about that lad of yours? He seems to be a bit of a handful.'

'He's just young and full of life,' Joan replied, loyally. 'He's an exceptionally bright boy, is Simeon, so he easily gets bored.'

John raised an eyebrow.

'He's playing with a friend today,' Joan informed him, hoping that she sounded as casual as possible. The reality was that she had had to ring round nearly everyone in Simeon's class before finally finding someone who, after much entreating, had agreed to look after him today, but only today.

On her arrival at the medical centre that morning, early, she'd made a beeline for Elliot's office to ask if perhaps Simeon could come in and play in the common room on one of the computers for a couple of days but the reply had been in the negative without a moment's hesitation. Sorting out Simeon's arrangements in many ways was more of a worry than what was happening to Ivy, who was at least safe and secure and a great one for doing as she was told. Quite how child-care arrangements for the next couple of days were to be achieved, she had no idea but worse still was the prospect that when Ivy did come home, she could no longer be left to look after her grandson reliably. Was it any wonder her headaches were worse?

When she visited the hospital yesterday evening, the doctor on the ward had summoned Joan into her office. A charming lady, a Dr Helliwell, who had thick auburn hair cut in a neat bob and a face that looked as if she cared. Leaving Simeon to entertain Ivy (and eat not just her grapes and sweets but those belonging to the patient in the next bed), Joan felt her stomach churning as she listened to what the doctor had to say. Yes, Ivy was very much better. The antibiotics had really helped. Her blood tests were better than they had been – her kidneys weren't one hundred per cent but nothing to worry about and apart from a rather enlarged heart, her chest x-ray was clear. All good news but that was where it stopped. Everyone's concern was for Ivy's mental state. The diagnosis of an early dementing process was irrefutable. Despite her physical improvement, she was still significantly more bewildered than they'd hoped for. The consultant psychiatrist with a particular interest in the elderly had been to review her. There might be an improvement, but this was doubtful. She was to be reviewed in the clinic.

Dr Helliwell's kind face had turned to one of concern. She had wanted to know about the circumstances at home, who was there, what help there was and would they need additional help as the situation was going to be hard and deteriorate over time, possibly quickly. Had Joan made arrangements to have control of Ivy's finances? It might just be possible at the moment to take out a Lasting Power of Attorney but she would need to move quickly on that one. When the dementia was worse, it would not be possible to be sure that Ivy understood what was going on and a Court of Protection order would have to be set up and that took significantly longer.

Before she realised what she was saying, Joan had found herself painting a completely unrepresentative picture of a cosy family, a loving husband who bent over backwards to do as much as he could, Simeon helping all the time but not to the point where it interfered with his schoolwork and neighbours on either side whose generosity knew no bounds when it came to offers of help.

'And my boss is so sympathetic,' Joan had heard herself continue. 'He's happy for me to take what time off I need. I'm so lucky.'

The doctor had looked delighted to hear all this. She was far more used to hearing disturbing tales of isolation and vulnerability. What a refreshing change it made to come across such a close-knit family with good community support.

Joan, glad to escape, had walked thoughtfully back to Ivy's bed, just in time to stop Simeon from climbing into the one empty bed in the bay and spoiling the nice clean laundry.

It was going to be harder to convince Dr Britton, however, who had been to the house and come to his own astute conclusions.

'You need to be thinking ahead, Joan. It's not simply the rest of the school holidays, it's long term.'

'I'm sure we'll be fine. Once my mother is home, we can get back into a routine. The hospital have promised that to start with, a carer will pop in at lunchtime to make sure she has a hot drink and something to eat and then Simeon gets home from school about four and I'm home just after six.'

John ran his fingers through his hair. 'Simeon's a young boy, Joan. You can't expect him to be in charge of his grandmother. What if she had another fall? Perhaps we ought to be thinking of a more comprehensive package of care, with more people calling in during the day.'

'Oh dear, we don't want to be a nuisance to anyone. Mother'll be dreadfully confused by lots of different people calling in. She's never taken kindly to strangers. I'm sure Simeon can manage. He loves his granny to bits and...'

'I don't want to be unkind, Joan. I'm sure Simeon does love Ivy to bits but we've got to ensure that everyone is safe, as well looked after as they need to be and that there are safety nets in place, just in case.'

'I'd reduce my hours, but we desperately need the money. We live off my income almost exclusively apart from a little pension and of course the state pension that my mother gets.'

'Well, you'll be entitled to certain benefits as well now. Think about putting them to good use – pay for someone to come and sit in with Ivy perhaps. You'll need a regular break. There's no way that you can work full time and be a full-time carer in what's left of your day. You'll be exhausted in no time.'

Joan looked unconvinced. In all honesty, she wasn't over pleased with people examining the minutiae of her personal and private life but Dr Britton, she knew, had nothing but the best at heart. He spoke a lot of sense. Big changes were going to have to be made and there was nobody else apart from her to make the decisions. She was fooling herself if she thought that life could go back to as it had been, albeit a precarious state of affairs at best, when Ivy came home from hospital.

'I'm here to help, Joan. There isn't anyone who would find this an easy situation. Talk to me regularly about what's going on – don't bother with appointments and all the formality, just grab me when I'm passing or email me and let's try to stay one step ahead of the game, thereby avoiding a crisis as much as possible. As soon as she's home, I'll come and see Ivy and keep a close watch on her.'

Joan bit her bottom lip, listening intently as he continued.

'So here's the plan, you come and see me on Thursday and tell me what your thoughts are and what ideas you've had. And we'll have a word about your headaches, though I can't imagine that all this has helped.

'The other thing you must remember, is that nobody, however wonderful they might be, can be a twenty-four-hour carer, seven days a week, for anything other than a short space of time. You need your rest and time off in order to be able to do this. Think about this too when you're making your plans. I can give you the name of an organisation that will send in someone to sit for a couple of hours with Ivy, to give you a break. All right?'

Joan had more or less stopped listening half way through his speech of advice. This was far and away the best idea that Joan had heard yet. A review with Dr Britton, plus the holiest of grails – open access to Dr Britton. She knew for a fact that few were favoured with such treatment apart from the terminally ill, where such commitment was fairly temporary, whereas with Ivy – well, she could go on for years! Momentarily her fatigue evaporated. He had virtually promised to do home visits on a regular basis which would mean that he would have the opportunity to get to know Simeon better. The openings for many cups of tea – perhaps a glass of something stronger if it was in the evening – were seemingly endless and how wonderful was that?

Joan's cup continued to overflow as she returned to her seat in reception and was passed a call from Gary who said that Faye Britton wanted to speak to her. The little job for the tennis club was hers if she wanted it. She didn't need to think twice. Although something of a two-edged sword, the extra access to Dr Britton and some spare cash far outweighed the fact that she hated tennis and the extra work eating into her spare time, which might be even less than it had been once Ivy was home.

But Faye hadn't stopped there. 'If you ever find that you need a bit of extra work, Joan, I can always use a hand around the house.'

Faye had not discussed this last invitation with John. She had thought of it only that morning when he had gone to work and she had been wandering down the stairs, half hidden by the pile of dirty laundry from all the visitors that she was carrying. They had had help with the cleaning intermittently over the years but not since Faye had stopped working some five years ago. John had sympathetically said that there was no reason why they couldn't continue with someone but Faye had declined, rather feeling that she ought to do it herself now that she was supposedly a lady of leisure. Like many people though, who give up work, her days were full before she knew it and she wondered how she had ever had time to fit work in. Nowadays, if she wasn't playing tennis or pursuing one of her other hobbies, she liked to meet up with friends for coffee or tea and recently had had the inspirational idea of joining a walking group which she very much hoped that John would join also.

Hearing about Joan's plight had upset her. Joan was a loyal and hard-working member of the practice team and had been for years. There must be more ways in which they could help. Faye had even thought of suggesting that she look after Simeon for a while, a couple of times a week, but wisely decided that she had better discuss such a step with John before taking it any further.

Joan found it hard to convey her gratitude, without the others starting to wonder what on earth she was talking about. The last thing she wanted was for her work colleagues to get wind of her having problems and needing to be helped out.

Promising to meet with Faye in the early New Year, Joan ended the call and returned to the job in hand, feeling so elated that she booked appointments for Mr Eric Mitchell and his wife Elspeth for Dr Britton that afternoon. She was fully aware that they were away on a three-week skiing trip in North America as they had been boasting about it last week when they came in to see the nurse about something but it would give him some breathing space in what looked like it was going to be a long, arduous session.

Chapter Sixteen

While the bells rang out and drunken voices sang terrible renditions of Auld Lang Syne, Ivy was welcoming in the New Year in her own style and wetting the bed. She had returned from hospital that morning, having got chilled to the bone as the hospital transport had wound its way up and down dale, delivering other people first to remote locations and although she seemed to realise that she was home, she was far from settled in.

Joan had been at work in the morning but, on account of her having worked until close of play on Christmas Eve, had taken her turn for an early finish. Once she had left, Elizabeth, Gemma and Gary toasted each other with much larger glasses of sherry than they had been allowed one week earlier.

Luckily, she was home before Ivy arrived, picking up Simeon on the way, who had spent the day with the same friend, for once not having blotted his copy book on the first occasion. Now Joan had the prospect of a Bank Holiday, a day off (holiday owing) and the weekend, after which surely a routine would have been re-established and Simeon would be back at school. The plan was to beg the after-school club to let him back in, as she had told Dr Britton, even though she hadn't phrased it quite like this, if only temporarily and hopefully Ivy would be able to manage at home with the lunchtime carer popping in. It all sounded perilous at best but they had to try.

The afternoon was somewhat dysfunctional as Ivy was confused by the change of scene, having become used to a hospital environment and the humdrum routine. She was persuaded to eat a small tea – just a sandwich, the crusts of which she left and a small bowl of tinned fruit. Joan had helped her up to bed around nine and never before had a flight of stairs been such a struggle. It took them nearly half an hour. Ivy might be able to walk across the ward with a walking frame but a dozen or so stairs was an unprecedented hurdle. Somehow, by various pushings and pullings, along with numerous rests for them both to get their breath back, they were victorious in their trial and the final few steps to her bedroom seemed a doddle by comparison.

'Perhaps we ought to think about bringing your bed downstairs,' Joan panted.

'Not in a million years. I've gone upstairs to bed all my life and I'm not stopping now,' was the curt reply. 'I've got you to help me, so we'll manage.'

Joan rolled her eyes.

Ivy fell sideways into bed at this point and Joan, unable to bear the thought of yanking her up on her feet again for a trip to the bathroom, left her there, only to regret this move, three hours later. By the time Ivy was dry, in clean sheets and nodding off to sleep, the last thing on Joan's mind was celebrating. She had a piercing headache and was longing to go to bed too.

Simeon was still in the lounge. He had insisted – which meant that he had had a blood-curdling tantrum – that he wanted to stay up and see in the New Year but had fallen asleep before eleven and so Joan had covered him with his duvet and left him snoring, curled up in the chair. He was a heavy sleeper and doubtless out for the count until the morning.

It was hardly surprising that she felt unable to face tidying up, washing up or any other form of housework, so Joan simply checked on Simeon and gazed around the lounge feeling defeated. Her mother had been home for half a day and it felt like weeks. Quite how this was all going to work out – well, who knew? But it had to.

The next day, the first day of the New Year, was decidedly better, which Joan took to be a good omen. The sun was shining and there had been the predicted drop in temperature, bringing with it a sharp frost which made everywhere look silver edged and stunning.

Ivy had slept relatively well until seven, when she had needed a hand to get out of bed and to the bathroom, but at least this meant that Joan had had an uninterrupted sleep, albeit with one ear listening out, for several hours. As a result she felt quite refreshed and optimistic and she even hummed a little as she dressed and made her bed. She loved her bedroom. It was the one room that was hers and hers alone. Nobody else was allowed in here. Both Ivy and Simeon had to knock. A few months ago, Simeon had barged in unannounced while she was dressing and burst out laughing at the sight of her semi-naked body, so upsetting Joan that she had taken the unprecedented step of putting a lock on the door. Since then, nobody had been in except her. Unlike the rest of the house, she kept her room immaculate – a little haven that gave her the ability to escape from the unkindness of her world once in a while. She had taken considerably more care over the decoration also – it was amazing what you could find in charity shops – lovely throws, curtains that had been discarded but that still had years of wear in them, even a fabulous quilt for her bed, a myriad of tiny patchwork hexagons in greens and yellows. What patience someone must have had to create such an object of beauty! An achievement she could never aspire to. More to the point, why would anyone not want it? She stroked it affectionately, smoothing out the last crease. Duvets were all very well, but her preference every time was for sheets and blankets.

The walls were covered with photographs, each one in a different frame. She had seen something similar in one of the magazines that a patient had brought in, which ought to have been put out in the waiting areas but as there were plenty there already, Joan had appropriated a couple of copies for herself to read with her coffee or of an evening. Inspired, she took down the rather cheap and faded paintings that did absolutely nothing for her any more, leaving tell-tale signs on the wallpaper where they had hung and up went the photos, dozens of them, each one with a deep personal meaning, some just stuck with pins until she gradually found cheap frames for them in her customary rifling through charity shops and jumble sales.

Initially, she had thought this new arrangement a bit odd, as normally she wasn't a great one for extra things that needed dusting but as her collection grew, she mentally congratulated herself on what she felt was a huge success and rather artistic. She looked at her photographs several times a day and each time, without fail, a warm glow spread through her body. Happy photos, images that made her smile. Not just good memories but also promises of wonderful things to come. She mustn't forget that she had some more she wanted to put up. Perhaps she would find time later on that day to do this, but now she had to return to reality as Simeon was shouting at Ivy who was, thankfully, laughing loudly.

This room was the only place she needed to be able to come to. Her sanctuary. Never mind what Dr Britton said about time off, a few minutes here and she was always restored.

Between them, Joan and Simeon orchestrated the transfer of Ivy from bedroom to lounge, stopping at the bathroom en route, at which point Simeon was ordered into his bedroom and told 'not to look' by his grandmother. Like some convoluted tango for three, they danced downstairs. The amount of energy required to do this was phenomenal, leaving them gasping for breath and Joan gave mental thanks that she had agreed (reluctantly) to the provision of a commode for use in the hall, its practicality trumping its inelegance and anyway it was easily disguised with an old sheet. Another for the bedroom might be no bad thing, on reflection.

With Ivy safely deposited on the sofa and Simeon embarking on the construction of some very complicated-looking model, Joan was considering putting the kettle on, when there was a knock on the door.

'Whoever's that?' asked Ivy, pulling a cushion out from under her knees.

'I'll go and find out, shall I?' suggested Joan.

She dealt with several locks and opened the door.

'Good morning and Happy New Year!' a cheery John Britton greeted her. 'I thought I'd just pop in and see how your first night was. I do hope I'm not disturbing you.'

Joan's heart gave a lurch. This was the best-ever first foot she had had, even if he was a bit late and wasn't carrying a piece of coal or a half bottle of whisky.

'Oh, Dr Britton. How kind of you. Yes, yes, Happy New Year to you too. Come in. No, of course you're not disturbing us. I'm about to make a cup of tea. I hope you'll join us. I'm so sorry about the mess. I've not had a chance to tidy yet. Ivy's just up. We're doing fine. Everyone had a good night's sleep! Not much in the way of celebrating but we're not ones to make a fuss over Hogmanay. Sorry, I'm gabbling!'

'That all sounds most promising. Well done, all of you.'

'Come in,' Joan repeated, 'let me take your coat. It's quite bitter out there today, isn't it? What a change! Now, you go into the lounge and chat to my mother and I'll bring you a nice cup of tea. I know just how you like it and we've some lovely biscuits too.'

'No biscuits for me,' John interrupted her, patting his stomach, determined to stick to his resolution. He saw Joan's face fall a little. 'But that cup of tea would be most welcome.'

Joan beamed and scurried into the kitchen, while John opened the lounge door, tried to ignore the chaos and find a place to sit down near Ivy.

'Hello Ivy,' he began.

'Who are you?' was the reply.

Simeon laughed. 'Don't be silly, it's the doctor, Granny! You are funny sometimes.'

'Of course it's the doctor. My glasses must need cleaning. How are you, doctor?'

It was John's turn to laugh. 'That's my line!' he smiled. 'You're looking well, Ivy, much better than when I last saw you. How do you feel?'

'Well, I'll be glad to get home, but I do feel quite well.'

'Excellent. How's the appetite? Are you drinking plenty – that's most important.'

'Yes, all of that. I'm not big eater at best but look, here's Joan with a drink for us now.'

If John realised that Joan was making use of her best china cups, he said nothing but gratefully accepted his drink as she passed it to him, standing firm on the offer of biscuits, feeling very proud of his achievement. Secretly he also felt what an uphill struggle this new diet was going to be as after only a few hours, he was already heartily sick of it. Faye's reaction when he had made his nutritional resolution known over breakfast was one of such delight mingled with relief that he was determined to succeed, come what may.

They made small talk for a while, as they drank, Ivy joining in from time to time, Simeon came over, uncharacteristically, to John and asked him to help with his model building.

'Goodness,' pronounced John after looking at the instructions, 'this is complicated. Let me see now. This bit goes here like this and that bit there. It's tricky but,' there was a satisfying snap, 'there you go.'

'Thanks,' Simeon grabbed the pieces and returned to the rest of the bits on the floor.

Joan simpered maternally. 'He's a very gifted boy,' she cooed. 'You're very honoured. He'd not go to most people to ask for help. He must like you a lot. Usually he has to settle for me and I'm useless at building models.'

'I'm sure you're not,' John commented chivalrously. He sneaked a glance at his watch and then drained his tea. 'So tell me, do you think you're going to be able to manage?'

'Please, let me get you more tea.' Almost snatching his cup and saucer, without waiting for an answer, lest he decline, she was out of the room and back before he knew it.

'Here you are. Nice and hot! Now, where were we? Oh I know...'

Joan sat down again and cleared her throat. She had been waiting for this and was well rehearsed. 'Yes. I won't say it's going to be easy but the hospital persuaded me to have a carer to come in each morning to get Mother up and downstairs as well as the one at lunchtime, at least to start with to see how we get on. They start the day after tomorrow. That'll be a big help as it will mean I can get Simeon off to school to breakfast club and then get to work. Of course I'll be here in the evenings. Oh, and we've got one of those alarm systems – or we will have when someone comes in tomorrow – you know the ones, Mother has a pendant around her neck which she presses if she needs help and then I'll be contacted. Oh, and I'm sure the commode in the hall is going to prove to be a boon. One in the bedroom might be an idea as well. I shall ring social services in the morning. I've the number of a lady who I can ring if I need anything.'

To John, the plan sounded flawed at best. So much depended on Ivy and whether she was able to cope with being on her own for hours at a time. Also whether Ivy remembered to keep her pendant on. Many was the patient he had met in the past who either forgot or didn't bother, not expecting to need it. But, there was an outside chance that it would work, for a short time and give Joan the opportunity to prepare for Ivy's certain deterioration.

From experience, John had seen many times how relatives dealt with dementia in the family. Some bailed out at the first hurdle, wanting their nearest and dearest in a home, where specialised nursing was available and where they could visit as it suited them. A neat solution but one that inevitably was followed by guilt that the family could have done more.

Others bent over backwards and beyond to keep their relative at home and many times this worked well, the patient being in familiar surroundings but needing often huge amounts of care input from outside agencies.

Whatever the choice, John knew that as often as feasible, people had to be allowed to try plans out before deciding if they were successful or not. It didn't take a genius to see that Joan was desperate to cope if she possibly could and so she needed to try, otherwise she would never forgive herself for not having given it her best shot. His job, as her GP, was to monitor the situation closely, try to stay one step ahead and hope for the best.

Chapter Seventeen

A month passed and a rather smug John found that he was able to get comfortably into a tweed sports jacket (and do up the buttons with ease) that he had not worn for many years. Likewise, a shopping trip to Harrogate had been necessary for the purchase of new trousers, two sizes smaller and, while he was there, Faye had taken advantage of the fact that he was actually in a clothes shop and had him stock up on three new shirts and a couple of jumpers.

His new physique had not been easily acquired, at least to begin with. His very soul seemed to scream for sugary foods. A piece of fruit and some yoghurt did not, however hard he tried, have the same satisfaction degree that crumble and custard did, or jam roly poly, or steamed syrup sponge, or cheesecake...the list not only went on and on but round and round in his head when he lay in bed at night, his stomach rumbling. Though the craving for sugar was at times nearly unbearable, at least, if he were honest, most of the time he didn't feel hungry. Faye had decided that he was allowed healthy portions of meat, chicken or fish and plenty of vegetables, jacket potatoes, brown rice, brown pasta, often preceded by a warming home-made soup to fill as many nooks and crannies in her husband's stomach as possible.

Like many diets, it was the beginning that was the hardest. Now, more or less on an even keel and taking care never to walk past the front window of Delicious where the cakes were on display, he was starting to see the results and the positive feedback from this was keeping him going. He was secretly proud of his new, more svelte physique. Patients had commented favourably, his colleagues, especially Ellie were well impressed and Joan had even come to see him to interview him about his new lifestyle for another article in her newsletter. She had asked what seemed like a million more questions, carefully noting down his replies and taken a lot more photos. For comparison, she had explained, which puzzled him. For sure he had lost some weight but not like those photos where people stand in one leg of the trousers they used to wear because they are so transformed. All he had done was get a bit trimmer. He wanted to lose another half a stone, if possible, and with a sinking heart had bought a static bicycle and rowing machine which were now set up in one of the spare bedrooms, ready for his exercise regime to begin. Any day now, he told his conscience. It was simply a matter of finding the time.

There was no denying that he felt a lot better. Whether this was because he was now doing something positive about the diabetes and 'embracing the diagnosis' (one of Ellie's phrases) which he had tried unsuccessfully to sweep under a carpet in his brain was a matter for debate but he felt in control of his life and very positive. Sadly this feeling did not extend to his job where he continued to be pelted on a daily basis with change and new protocols, some of which made him want to scream and walk out of the door without further ado, because he knew that they were idiotic.

'Why do they never ask the people who are actually doing the bloody job?' he repeatedly was heard to say as he stomped round the medical centre, flapping print-outs of emailed documents as though swatting flies.

When they were in the common room, perhaps at coffee time or before afternoon surgery, he often peeped surreptitiously at his colleagues to see how they were coping. Clare inevitably looked harassed and pale. Whilst motherhood had in some ways calmed her and given her other priorities in her life, she still took everything to heart and tried to be too much to too many patients. John suspected, correctly as it happened, that she was trying for another child with her husband David. He had seen her taking folic acid tablets with her coffee, which was now decaffeinated and when they last met for a post-surgery drink in the local pub, she had asked for an orange juice instead of her usual glass of wine.

Ellie and Ed were the stalwarts. Ellie, as ever, juggling the many aspects of her life seemingly effortlessly, bringing up the twins, as much in love with her husband Ian as she was when they first met and she was still as beautiful, though now in a slightly more mature way. Ed was one of life's copers. He seemed unflappable. Throw anything at him and he'd sort it out and amazingly would still be smiling at the end.

Good, solid, reliable partners. And good friends too. Often hard to come by in this day and age. How lucky had he been?

And then there was Faith. Talented, clever but with so little self-belief, outside of work. She lived with Rob, one of their past registrars and despite his constant support and their very solid relationship – John suspected wedding bells before long – she continued to binge on food and battle with her weight, as she had for years. John knew that she thought it was still her secret but he also knew that she was capable of emptying the biscuit tin when nobody else was in the common room. He'd seen her leave Delicious with bags of cakes which had mysteriously disappeared by the time she got back to the medical centre, having specifically taken the long route and, saddest of all, he had heard the retching noises as he had passed by her consulting-room door, forcing herself to vomit when she had thought she was alone. He knew that she longed to be a partner. Would the others choose her when he left?

He wasn't there to offer suggestions. It was their choice and he had every confidence in them to make the correct one. Once he left, that would be it. A job done to the best of his ability but one that was over.

Tick.

He had no intention of being one of those people who can't let go of their job, who keep popping back to the workplace to see how everyone is and what's going on, unable to cut that final strand of some invisible umbilical cord. He would of course stay in touch socially and it was virtually impossible to walk across the market square without bumping into more than one patient he knew so he had no doubt whatsoever that those with a penchant for gossip would keep him up to speed.

The future indeed was looking rosy, he thought, reaching into his bag and taking out the lunchbox, so lovingly prepared by Faye. As he surveyed the contents, which looked delectable, those with the keenest of hearing might possibly have heard him utter a wistful sigh.

Across town, Joan's future was looking far from rosy. Picking out the positives, Ivy seemed pleased to be at home and was now aware where she was. The incontinence pads had been a boon. So had the extra commode.

Considerably outweighing these were the facts that Ivy hated the carers and was rude to them, refusing to let them help when it came to anything of a more personal nature and her dementia was noticeably worse. Few nights passed without her shouting out for Joan, who consequently felt chronically worn out and approaching her wits' end, the knock-on effect of which made it harder and harder to deal with Simeon, who was quick to take advantage.

His head teacher had agreed, after hearing the circumstances at home, substantially modified by Joan so that it sounded as if she was in total control, to let Simeon attend breakfast club and after-school club, with the sole proviso that this was the last chance saloon and one step out of line would mean exclusion for life. Thank goodness for that, Joan had thought and she had sat Simeon down on his bed and spent over half an hour explaining to him how important it was that he behaved from now on. Wide eyed and innocent, Simeon had promised his mother the earth, hoping for some recompense in the form of treats – chocolate and sweets (good) or money (even better).

When, after the first fortnight, he had received no material gain whatsoever and none looked to be forthcoming, his resolve, which was already wavering, evaporated. He had started fighting with other boys, bullying one of the girls and throwing food, mostly soggy breakfast cereal. Joan had been confronted and before she realised what was happening, she had burst into tears, an event she was bitterly ashamed of but one which engendered such sympathy in the head teacher that it was agreed that they would try a further two weeks but that really was it, unless there was a huge improvement.

Simeon seemed to be hell bent on a path to self-destruction. Despite warnings, bribes and threats of sanctions from his mother and teachers, his appalling behaviour continued regardless and, as warned, he was asked to leave with effect from the end of the week.

Joan was beside herself. What was she to do? Simeon needed some guidance from a father figure – he might just listen for once. It was perfectly clear that he had no respect at all for his mother and was unlikely to change overnight.

Taking him to see Dr Britton for a consultation was one idea but one that was instantly dismissed. In the formal setting of the consulting room, it might appear that she thought Simeon had a problem, which, of course, she would not want Dr Britton to know about. Unfortunately, though true to his word and visiting on a weekly basis, Dr Britton had always popped in at the end of his morning rounds, when Joan had managed to get her lunch break to coincide and thereby provide an inaccurate but optimistic report on the situation. Which was fine apart from the fact that he was always in a rush and never had time for a cup of tea. Also he never saw Simeon and it was clear to Joan that they had felt some sort of mutual bond, as evidenced by Simeon asking for help with his model. Joan felt so frustrated as she tried to plan. Dare she ask if Dr Britton could visit in the evenings? There would be so much more time to talk and he would be more than welcome to sit down and eat with them. She might even open a bottle of wine... It would seem like they were a family...

What to do?

Simeon was capable of doing the short walk home from school on his own but then he'd be in the house with Ivy for perhaps three hours before she came home. The potential for chaos did not bear thinking about.

The option for her to reduce her hours did not exist. They needed every penny she earned and she so wanted to take up Mrs Britton's offer of doing a bit of housework for them.

Last week they had met with their social worker who, hearing warning bells, had suggested day care for Ivy, who was now getting to the stage where she really ought not to be left alone for so long. What a wonderful help that was, thought Joan, lifting a huge weight off her troubled mind but it did nothing for the Simeon dilemma.

Joan's brain hurt from the constant thinking. Every time she came up with a plan, it was flawed and had to be consigned to the bin. Sleepless night followed sleepless night. She was ratty and distracted at work and suffered the humiliation of being taken to one side by Elliott and asked what was wrong.

Eventually, only one option remained, long shot though it was. It needed a lot of courage on her part but then he had said ring any time.

With a thumping heart, she swallowed hard and picked up the telephone. A male voice answered after a few rings. Various pleasantries were exchanged.

'Can we meet, please?' asked Joan, trembling as she waited for the answer.

'Thank you. Saturday is fine...one o'clock...The Nosebag cafe? Yes I know where it is. See you then.'

John was rowing down the Amazon. At least that was what he was imagining. He had already navigated the Thames and the Pacific Ocean, escaping a shark attack and admiring a school of leaping dolphins. Anything, to relieve the boredom of the rowing machine. He'd been on it now for five whole minutes and the monotony made it feel like five hours. How on earth did people manage to keep going? Well, there was one thing in its favour. He was wringing wet with sweat, which must be a sign that it was doing him good.

Enough was enough. He got up, legs like jelly, and climbed onto the static bike, ready to start le Tour de Yorkshire.

'Don't do too much first time,' advised Faye, putting her head around the door and doing her best not to laugh at the sight before her. He was dressed in shorts and a vest, towel round his neck and a headband.

'Just a few more minutes,' he gasped.

'You're doing wonderfully. I'm so proud of you.'

Faye perched on the end of the bed, putting her pile of dirty laundry down.

'It's so mind-blowingly boring,' John complained.

'We can put the little television in here, if you like, then you can watch that.'

'It might help, I guess. Phew, that's enough for today.' He rested his head on the handlebars. 'I hadn't realised how unfit I was,' he wailed.

Faye gave him a quick kiss. 'You know as well as I do that it'll take a bit of time. When the weather's better we can get bikes perhaps. Ed'll give us some easy routes to do.'

'Let's get a tandem and bags me sit at the back.'

Faye laughed. 'Go and shower! You smell terrible! But I love you to bits for all that you're doing.'

He threw his headband at her. 'I couldn't do it without you.'

The telephone rang.

'Can you get that, please?' asked Faye. 'It's nearly always for you and I must get these in the washer.'

'Sure,' was the reply as John went into their bedroom.

She heard the shower start shortly afterwards and was pleased to be joined by a clean, sweet-smelling husband who obligingly filled the kettle and switched it on.

'The trouble with exercise,' he mused, 'is that it makes you hungry. Well, it does me.'

'Well that's fine, so long as you eat something sensible.'

'That's the problem. Hey ho, dry oatcakes, where are you?'

'In that tin, no the one next to that one you've got your hand on. That's the one.'

'Thanks. Oh by the way, are you playing tennis on Saturday?'

'Yes, weather permitting. Is that okay with you?'

'Of course. You know I love you to play whenever you want. I lose track a bit in the winter. I'm popping into Harrogate to meet a friend. Do you want tea or coffee?'

Chapter Eighteen

'Get yourself dressed, Simeon, have a wash please and put on your clean tee shirt and jeans,' Joan ordered.

'Why?' His eyes did not move from the television where cartoon characters were chopping each other's limbs off. He was still in his pyjamas.

'Because I say so and we're going to Harrogate to get you some new school uniform. Your jumper's a disgrace and your trousers are flapping round your calves. They look more like long shorts.'

'Don't want to. I'm watching this.'

Purposefully, Joan strode across the room, snatched the remote control before Simeon realised what she was doing and killed the television. She faced him, a 'don't mess with me' expression on her face. 'Bad luck. You don't have a choice, sadly. This is the only chance we've got to go, while Granny's at the day centre. We'll go out for lunch though…'

Simeon cast her a look and she knew he was wavering. 'Can I have chips?'

'You can have whatever you want, within reason, if you're good.'

Anything, anything to get him to comply.

'And pudding?'

'All right.'

'And some sweets to bring home – for Granny, of course.'

'We'll see. Maybe something nice for our supper. Now off you go, we're leaving in ten minutes.'

Simeon contemplated the deal for a couple of moments but seemed convinced and disappeared to get dressed. Joan followed him upstairs and shut her bedroom door firmly behind her. Earlier she had laid out a dress she didn't often wear, plain burgundy and safe, even a bit old fashioned but a sparkly scarf would liven it up nicely. Sheer black tights, a change from the thick knit ones she tended to favour in the winter and a pair of black court shoes with sensible heels. There was walking to be done so anything more frivolous was a non-starter.

Clothes changed, she surveyed her reflection in the mirror and applied a modest amount of makeup, before rubbing off most of the lipstick, which she knew she never got quite right anyway. Overall, she was pleased with the result. She felt that she looked like a confident, independent woman and not – if she was honest – unattractive. Perhaps though, the dress was a bit sombre. It would have to do.

She performed a twirl in front of her photographs, who smiled back at her, approvingly.

Any more thoughts were dissipated by Simeon banging on the door, yelling that not only was he ready but he was also hungry and no, before she even suggested it, a stupid banana would not do and anyway there were none left as Granny had eaten the last one for breakfast.

Joan unlocked her door and came out.

'You look smart.' Simeon was a little taken aback. Suddenly suspicious, he asked 'Are you sure we're going shopping?'

'Of course we are and thank you for noticing. I thought I'd like to look smart.' Joan reached out to give him a hug but he recoiled as usual, so she shrugged. 'Let's go. Won't it be lovely to spend some time together?'

Luckily, Joan did not see the lack of conviction all over her son's face.

The journey was actually quite pleasant. Shafts of sunlight broke through the clouds and they spotted a few tiny lambs cavorting in the fields. In her excitement, Joan chattered away relentlessly and Simeon joined in. When she was in a good mood and not moaning at him or complaining about being tired all the time and having headaches, his mother was good company and he liked talking to her. And she didn't just chat, they played games as they drove along, I- spy, making words from the letters on other cars' registration plates and she laughed, out loud, as their suggestions became sillier and so did he.

Her good humour continued, helped by there being an empty parking space in the car park opposite the school-uniform shop, where they had the undivided attention of a rather fussy sales lady. Their straightforward purchases were made in record time, Simeon being obliging with trying on trousers until the correct size was found – slightly long and therefore allowing room for growth.

Joan checked her watch as they left the shop, bags in either hand. 'I think it's lunchtime now, don't you?'

'Yes! Where shall we go?'

'I know just the place,' his mother replied. 'Come on.'

They wended their way along the crowded pavements and across the precinct until finally Joan pushed open the door to a small café. Just as well, as Simeon was on the point of complaining that he couldn't walk any further. It was very popular and the tables were jammed close together. They were covered with cheerful pale blue checked cloths made of real cotton and on each was a small vase of flowers, blue and yellow and plastic but quite realistic until you looked closely. The waitresses, who looked run off their feet, were still smiling which was a good sign, together with the encouraging smell of chips and a very interesting array of cakes and desserts on the counter. Simeon was happy to give it the thumbs-up apart from the sad fact that every table seemed to be occupied by equally hungry shoppers.

'It's too busy,' Simeon yanked his mother's arm. 'There's nowhere to sit. Oh, I'm so hungry. Now we'll have to find somewhere else and I'm fed up. You've made me walk all this way for nothing. It's all your fault.'

'Shut up, Simeon,' Joan turned to him. 'I've spotted a space, so let's go and sit down. Look, over there.'

In the corner of the café- were two empty chairs at a table, occupied by a good-looking, middle-aged man who was studying the menu.

'But there's someone sitting there.'

'It's busy, we need to make do. We can share.'

'I don't want to.'

Joan settled into one of the chairs and gesticulated for Simeon to do the same. The man watched them with interest. Simeon stuck his tongue out at him. The man laughed and returned the gesture.

'Simeon, don't do that,' Joan reprimanded him. 'Here's the menu, what do you want? I'm sorry about that,' she turned to the man.

'Apology accepted. I'd recommend the double cheeseburger and chips. That's what I'm going to order. With lots of tomato ketchup and a portion of onion rings on the side. Then for dessert I'm thinking about the apple pie, hot with a double scoop of vanilla ice cream. Oh, and a pot of tea.'

Simeon glowered at him, mouth slightly open, flummoxed. It was precisely what he was going to ask for, apart from the pot of tea. The man raised his eyebrows and stared back, a slight tilt to his head, a hint of an air of challenge in his expression. Not many people did that and Simeon was perturbed.

'Mum, can we move to another table? I don't like that man. He's rude.'

Joan sighed. The time had come.

'Simeon, we're staying where we are. This man is your father. Hello, Greg, how are you? I barely recognised you. Simeon – say hello.'

Chapter Nineteen

'I had to do it.'

Ivy and Joan were sitting together in the lounge, drinking cocoa and dunking biscuits, with a view to making their way to bed in the near future.

'Do what, dear?' Ivy asked.

'Get in touch with Greg. I told you. No matter how I tried, there was nobody else that I could ask to help. He put his contact details in the Christmas card he sent. Maybe it was "a sign".'

'Then that was the best idea. He is Simeon's father after all.' Ivy had one of her increasingly rare moments of clarity, adding as an afterthought, 'Bastard.'

'I know you never liked him. But it's only right and fair that he gets to know his son and vice versa as well. It might be beneficial for Simeon. He barely uttered a word while we had lunch.'

'He's been very quiet since you got back too. I was worrying that he was coming down with a bug.'

'He's suddenly got a lot to think about. It's really knocked him for six. I'll try and have a good chat to him tomorrow, when he's had a bit of time to mull over today.'

'Then what happens next?'

'Well, with Simeon being so tongue-tied, Greg and I at least had a chance to speak. They're going out for the afternoon tomorrow, the two of them and if it goes well then Greg will help me by doing the school run and also look after him until I finish work. You'd think differently of him now, Mother. He's improved with age, looks wise.

Almost handsome apart from a horrible beard. He's remarried, you know. He showed me a photo of her. Rosie, she's called. She's a teacher now and looked nice enough. Nothing special. Simeon will meet her tomorrow. It's an awful lot for the boy to take in all at once. It must have been a terrible shock for him. I've always been so dismissive when he has asked about his father, not that he's done that very much and then out of the blue I take him shopping and lo and behold, guess who we meet? I feel guilty about doing it all so fast, but there's no option.'

'You've done the right thing,' Ivy endorsed. 'He needs a father figure, as I'm always telling you. A man to look up to. No, I never liked him. He wasn't right for you, dear, I knew all along. Is there any more of this drink? It's very pleasant.'

'Yes, of course,' Joan carried on talking as she took Ivy's mug from her and went into the kitchen, raising her voice as she ran the tap to fill the kettle. 'What I'm really hoping is that Simeon and his dad will get on well and then Simeon can have some sleepovers there at weekends. Then I can take up Dr Britton's offer of a few hours work at his house. The money would be such a help. When I put the tennis club details on the computer earlier this month, I noticed that Mrs Britton plays every Saturday and Sunday, so it would be ideal for me to clean then, while the house is empty.'

She stirred the contents of Ivy's mug. 'Oh, I so hope that this works out for all of us. I just want what's best for Simeon, you know.'

There was no reply.

'Mother? Did you hear me? What do you think?'

But Ivy was nodding, chin resting on her chest, clumps of congealed crumbs across her bosom, half a biscuit still clutched in one hand.

Joan gently nudged her awake. 'Come on, let's get you upstairs. It's time for bed.'

She watched the bemused look on her mother's face as she struggled to work out where she was and who Joan was.

'Sorry, dear. I was only thinking. Now, help me up to bed and then you can tell me all about what you did today. Was it busy at the medical centre?'

For a fraction of a second, Joan felt totally alone. It was so difficult to cope with the variability of Ivy's condition. One minute she seemed fine, the next – as some of her work colleagues had been heard to say – away with the fairies. She really didn't want Greg to get too involved. If he helped with Simeon then that would be perfect and yes, it would be beneficial for Simeon to get to know his father but as far as Ivy was concerned, there was no need for him to know anything apart from the bare bones. She suspected the sight of him might really upset Ivy, whose memory for the distant past was typically intact, so they needed to be kept well apart.

How hard was all this going to be? Juggling all these conundrums at once? She wished that she had a confidante, a caring, listening ear and a shoulder to cry on. Everyone else seemed to have one but her. It didn't seem fair but as she was on the brink of falling into a trough of self-pity, she remembered she did have an ally, one she was able to call on any time she needed. John Britton! Excitingly, when her plans all dovetailed together – and she was confident that they would – the opportunities to spend more and more time with him were breathtakingly awesome.

Chapter Twenty

John Britton had never been one to make a big deal of Valentine's Day. He maintained that there was no need for a special day to tell Faye that he loved her. He told her that most days anyway and often bought her flowers, well, occasionally at best. There was no way that he was going to bow to the pressure of commercialisation and pay inflated prices for red roses, chocolates and candlelit dinners. Neither was there a chance in hell that he might be spotted rifling through the reams of red, slushy cards, oozing sentimentality, that were to be found in the local post office.

Faye was completely content with this arrangement, concurring with all his opinions. Many years ago, she had sent him one but that was when she wanted him to notice her, even though it wasn't signed of course. It had been a bit of a giveaway when she had handed it to him personally, without even trying to pretend it was from anyone else. Once they were a couple and knew that that was the way they were going to stay, it was by mutual agreement that cards or any other form of gift were deemed unnecessary. A nice evening in, a good home-cooked meal and maybe a bottle of wine was perfect for the two of them. In essence, an evening not unlike many other evenings they spent in each other's company.

So, to all intents and purposes, John had no idea whatsoever that it actually was Valentine's Day. To him, it was the same as any other work day and he got up, had his - please note - porridge and fruit for breakfast, kissed Faye tenderly on the cheek and tootled off to work, taking the same route as always, rather dreading what may lie in store for him. He had lain awake a large part of the night worrying about a patient's blood results, which were difficult to make sense of but very definitely abnormal and the questions were, what needed to be done and with what degree of urgency? The patient had looked unwell and he had debated in his mind whether to admit her to be on the safe side. It was so difficult these days admitting patients. The hospital doctors on call always seemed to put up barriers and tell general practitioners that it didn't sound necessary. So he then decided to wait for her bloods results, which had done nothing more than throw him into a greater state of indecision. He would ring the on-call consultant before he started surgery and get some advice. Not the best start to his day but an increasingly common one. Nowadays he and the others asked for so many more blood tests than they used to, in part due to patient pressure and fear of complaints which was fine but had an annoying tendency to throw up mild abnormalities which were probably nothing but of course had to be followed up, all the while generating a considerable amount of anxiety for both patient and doctor.

His job was a strange entity. Take recently for example. He'd had a series of really tricky diagnostic dilemmas, some other patients who had needed a lot of time but weirdly, he had had in every one of his surgeries, patients booked in who had failed to attend, thereby freeing him up to deal with the difficulties and still not finishing too late. This was a phenomenon he was not used to. Of course, they all had occasional patients who didn't turn up but he knew he was popular with an incredibly faithful following and those patients rarely missed the opportunity to see him. If they did then they wrote lengthy letters saying how sorry they were or phoned the surgery to beg forgiveness.

However, he was not going to complain. He had mentioned it to Ellie and Ed who had told him to enjoy it while it lasted. Like as not, this good phase would be replaced by one of craziness before too long.

That day appeared to be no different. The consultant on call agreed to see his patient that morning but reassured him that there had been no need to admit her earlier. One thing less to worry about, thought John, after phoning the patient, who was surprised, touched and extremely grateful to be rung so early by her general practitioner, and making arrangements for her to attend the assessment unit at eleven.

Head cleared of his biggest worry, John ploughed on with his surgery, feeling almost embarrassed when his fifth and sixth patients did not attend, giving him enough time to sneak up to the common room for an extra cup of coffee. He twiddled his thumbs while he looked at his colleagues' lists. No one else seemed to be having the same good fortune as he. Clare was, not uncommonly, running very late indeed. Guiltily, he rang through to reception and spoke to Gary.

'Yes, Dr Britton? Can I help?'

Before he heard the reply, the receiver was snatched from his hand by Joan.

'Senior partner, senior receptionist,' she hissed. Gary looked completely taken aback. When Joan wasn't looking he mouthed at Elizabeth, 'What's all that about?'

'Yes, Dr Britton. Joan speaking...' Her best voice.

'Can I see any patients for anyone? Dr Jennings for example. I'm sitting here doing nothing. There are queues of folk waiting for the others.'

'Oh, don't you worry. The demand for appointments is quite low today. Very few house-call requests and none for you. Make the most of it, Dr Britton. Can I bring you a coffee?'

'No thanks, Joan.'

'Tea then?'

'No thanks.'

' Well, if you're sure...'

'I am, Joan. I'll crack on with some paperwork.'

'I'll bring in some prescriptions for you to sign and just have a little tidy up then.'

'There's no need...'

But she had hung up.

He finished his surgery before time as the final patient didn't materialised either. A feat not accomplished since, well, in truth, he couldn't actually remember. Feeling a bit stupid, he waited in his consulting room watching on the computer as the others, one by one, some more quickly than others, brought their morning sessions to a conclusion. Only then did John think it appropriate that he went up to the common room. This free time made him feel a tad empty, if he were honest.

Ellie, in a knee-length dress of ice blue was making a hot chocolate, chatting furiously into her mobile phone which she had wedged between her ear and shoulder, thus freeing up both hands. She waved the coffee jar at John, who nodded. Call ended, she brought their drinks over to the table around which they all sat.

'That was school. Lydia's got a high fever and vomited and Virginia's complaining of a feeling sick. Obviously coming out in sympathy. They've both been given some paracetamol but I'd better go and pick them up. I could tell by the tone of the school nurse's voice that she doesn't want them there. Luckily it's my half day and Ian's off tomorrow. How's your day going?'

John slurped his coffee, feeling rather awash with fluids and wishing he could have a chocolate biscuit.

'Odd,' he replied emphatically. 'Another three non-attenders. Two of them were that couple who usually see you, Mr and Mrs Bairstow. I don't think I've seen either of them for years, so why they'd booked in with me is a mystery.'

'Odd is right,' agreed Ellie. 'I know for a fact that the Bairstows are on a cruise in the Caribbean at the moment. Mrs Bairstow rang the surgery yesterday from the boat, asking if it was okay for her to go scuba diving. Why on earth would they have made an appointment for while they were away? I suppose it's just an oversight. But it's not like them, I have to say. He used to be in the RAF and runs his life like clockwork.'

'Well, at least I can help you out with visits so that you can get off and pick up the twins.'

'That would be great. Thanks, John.'

She looked him seriously. 'I'll really miss you when you retire. We all will. But you're such a great senior partner and support. You always have been. To say nothing of being a fabulous friend.'

John tried to cover his embarrassment. 'Oh, you'll find someone to take my place and forget all about me.'

Ellie shook her head. 'No, nobody will take your place. You've wonderful, old-school ideals, which we still need today. I doubt we'll find someone with a similar work ethic.'

'Oh, now you're making me blush!' he laughed.

Ellie went round to him and gave him a hug. Every word she had said was heartfelt. 'And I might cry! What a silly pair we are!'

Fortunately, before they both ended up in tears, they were joined by Ed, Clare and Faith, all three gagging for a drink and some camaraderie. There was a general bustle of activity around the kettle before all five of them were seated round the table, all logged on to their laptops and making a start on booked telephone calls and dealing with messages.

There was a light tap at the door and Joan came in, bearing the post. She walked round them in turn, handing out various forms to be filled in, last-minute requests for repeat prescriptions and a couple of letters from patients wanting to let their doctor know in advance about problems they were going to come in and discuss.

'Dr Bonnington, there's your usual Valentine's card from old Mr Shepherd. I recognise his writing, plus he's put his name and address on the back of the envelope.'

All the doctors laughed.

She hesitated when she came to John. 'Nothing for you, Dr Britton, apart from this and if I'm not mistaken – though of course it's no business of mine – the red envelope suggests that you too might be the lucky recipient of a Valentine's card. Plus if size is anything to go by, there's someone out there who is very fond of you, very fond indeed.'

She left the room, leaving the doctors gawping at a huge envelope, with childish writing on the front, clearly an attempt at disguise. There was no stamp, no postmark. Obviously it had been left at reception.

'Open it,' said Clare, longing, as the others were, to see what was inside.

'Do I have to?' he replied.

'Oh, yes,' was the cry, in unison.

'I'll do it later...'

'No! Now!' they all encouraged him.

The envelope was not sealed. He passed the card round with horror.

'Oh my goodness, whoever sent this?'

'Faye?' suggested Faith.

'Not in a million years...'

Probably many people would have been delighted to receive the gigantic card, the front of which was awash with hearts and cute teddy bears, intertwined and hugging each other with enthusiasm.

'What does it say inside?' asked Ed, unable to contain his amusement, opening it.

'I hardly dare look...'

Ed gingerly opened the card. The entire interior was red. Written in the same childish handwriting that had been on the envelope was a short message,

'Never be sad, never be blue, always remember that I love you. My love will never go out of fashion, let's get together and share our passion.'

The last three words were underlined many times. A row of kisses and hand-drawn hearts followed. There was a moment's stunned silence before Faith snorted, precipitating simultaneous guffaws from the others and it was some time before any of them could manage to speak.

'Well! Which patient's responsible for that?' chuckled Clare, wiping her eyes. 'It sounds as if you need to be very careful, if you ask me. You've definitely got a secret admirer.'

'I haven't got the first clue,' John was genuinely bewildered.

'Of course, it might not be a patient...'

'I still have no idea.'

'It's certainly cheered us all up. In fact, I feel somewhat envious,' Ed pretended to sniff a little.

'Don't you think that there's something just a little bit scary about it, though?' asked Faith, looking worried.

'Why?'

'It's hardly subtle, is it?'

John patted her on the shoulder. 'I'm sure it's a jolly joke that someone's playing. I'll probably see a patient this afternoon or tomorrow who confesses and we'll have a good laugh about it.'

'I hope you're going to put it on your desk,' Ellie insisted.

'What? When it's this size? I hardly think so. I'd be invisible. No, I'll take it home with me. I can't imagine what Faye's going to say.'

All in considerably better spirits, they returned to the job in hand, before dividing up the house calls and letting Ellie get off to school as soon as she had finished. Ready to leave, John realised he had left his stethoscope in his room and, cursing slightly, he went to get it. On his desk was a small parcel, which when opened turned out to be a box of chocolates, a most expensive brand. There was a moment where he longed to rip of the packaging and indulge but curiosity out-won temptation.

He stopped at the reception desk on his way to the car park and asked where they had come from.

'Someone left them for you, Dr Britton,' Joan told him.

'Who?'

'I didn't see. It was Gary who was on the front desk.'

'And where's Gary?'

'On his break. He'll never remember. He's a memory like a sieve, that boy. I wish Elliott would have a word with him.'

John shrugged and left. Easing his car out of his designated parking place, he steered towards the exit, catching sight of Gary jogging back to work, most likely having been for an illicit cigarette around the corner.

He wound the window down. 'Gary,' he called.

'Oh, hello, Doc Britton. Don't worry, I'm just on my way back to work.'

'That's fine. I only wanted to ask who left that parcel for me this morning.'

'What parcel's that?' Gary was obviously puzzled.

'The one you put on my desk.'

Shaking his head, Gary coughed. 'That wasn't me, Doc. I haven't seen any parcels all day.'

'But Joan said you were on the front desk.'

'I was but I swear I never took in any parcels.'

John was in no doubt that he was being utterly honest. 'How peculiar. Never mind. Thanks for your time. I must get off now and get these visits done. See you this afternoon.'

Well, he thought. I'm no further forward than I was. Hey ho. It was nice of someone to think of me. What a shame I can't eat them but Faye will enjoy them. Now where's my first house call?

Chapter Twenty-one

The relationship between Simeon and his father was not progressing smoothly. Whilst the passage of years had resulted in a far more mature Greg who was keen to utilise his natural talent for being a father, it had done little to turn Simeon into the ideal son. This arrival of a male figure into his life that his grandmother so wanted, was unwelcome enough to start with, turning his cosy little life, where he was undisputedly in charge, upside down. All the more so this man, who answered back, had not only the ability to be equally rude but also – and worst of all – the audacity to say no. And how dare he appear after years of absence and feel that he had the right to start being the father he had never been.

After so long being looked after by his soft-as-butter mother and grandmother, who acquiesced to his every whim, the challenge that Greg presented was largely unwelcome but there was also something irritatingly intriguing about it. The same applied to his wife.

Rosie was a dumpy woman who, despite Joan's point of view, was in reality rather gorgeous in a doll-like way with curves in all the right places, huge blue eyes which were heavily made up and curly dark brown hair. She celebrated her size by wearing colourful clothes and smelled of perfume, which Simeon secretly found rather exciting. His mother smelled of cooking or fabric conditioner or ill people. She rarely wore 'real' perfume.

Rosie was welcoming and sanguine. Their house seemed huge, having four bedrooms and a garden at least five times the size of the one Simeon was used to. There was also a further unfamiliarity in the shape of a dog, Rex, a hotch potch of several breeds, who had come from the local rescue centre and had the unnerving habit of curling up his top lip and showing his teeth. Greg and Rosie assured Simeon that this was his way of smiling. Simeon was unconvinced but liked it when Rex came and sat on his lap and asked for his ears to be tickled.

Greg, keen to start off the way he intended to continue, had been quick to establish boundaries across which Simeon was not allowed to stray, much to the latter's annoyance as he had never experienced anything of the sort before. Rosie, whom Simeon had assumed would be as malleable as his mother, was also a force to be reckoned with and after the first couple of visits, he had returned home in the most foul of tempers and run up to his bedroom, slamming the door behind him with such vehemence that the whole house shook, screaming at the top of his voice that he never, ever wanted to see his father again.

Joan steeled herself against her son's diatribe of abuse, which was aimed at both her and Greg, though mainly her, and repeatedly told Simeon that this was non-negotiable. A tiny part of her felt sorry for her son and guilty for having inflicting this upset but she had needs too, so did Ivy and everyone of them had to make sacrifices in their lives to move forward.

After the first week, which, in short, was an unmitigated disaster, Greg was invited, albeit unwillingly, into the lounge for a cup of tea on the Friday evening, but no biscuits or cake. The atmosphere was very tense. Joan did her best to be a polite hostess, wanting the meeting to be over with as quickly as possible, ideally with the outcome of her choice. Ivy, in her usual spot on the sofa, was mystified. She knew that this man looked familiar but kept forgetting his name and where he slotted into her life and whether he was someone she liked or not. Her ambivalence was further complicated by Simeon's reaction to his presence. He came across as pleasant enough so what was so bad about him to make her beloved Simeon run out of the room and hide upstairs? Nobody was allowed to upset him. Not as long as she was there to protect him.

Greg sat uncomfortably on the edge of a chair, wishing Rosie was there as she always seemed to know what to say in awkward situations. He stirred his tea thoughtfully. He wasn't completely devoid of feelings towards Joan. The sight of her angular frame and worn- out face when they met in the cafe had shocked him. Time had not been kind to her but maybe in part he was to blame for this. Bringing up their son had clearly not been easy. He was relieved to see that she looked a little better today on her home territory, minimally more relaxed and had rather more colour about her. The decrepit state of the house did not escape his notice. A sad, world-weary ambience embraced him as he sat there; it wasn't just the building that needed some tender loving care but the occupants also.

Naively he had hoped that Simeon and he would be great friends from the word go. He got on famously with his friends' children and took it for granted that it would be the same with his own son. He was so looking forward to showing him off, introducing him to others, going on days out and enjoying time at home. Even helping with his homework. A happy vision had been conjured up in his mind of himself and Simeon, standing on the touchline at the local football match or poring over a book together, Simeon doing the work but being steered by a supportive father and getting praise from his teacher.

Never in a million years had he expected to be faced with a tyrannical, mulish boy, obstreperous at best, for whom the only way was his way and this was not up for discussion. Rosie had repeatedly told him to give it time, plenty of time. To remember how long it had taken Rex to settle in and he was a dog. That the poor boy must feel as though a runaway tram had driven through his life. From having no father that was ever spoken of to one that was alive and well in the space of time that it took to order a beefburger was a fairly daunting experience for anyone, especially when that someone was only nine years old.

'So, how have you got on?' asked Joan, in her best senior receptionist's voice.

Greg looked towards the door lest it opened and Simeon came in. 'To be honest, it's not quite what I imagined...' he began. 'He's quite a,' he searched for the right words, not wanting to offend, 'headstrong boy.'

Joan was dismissive. 'That's his natural confidence. He's very mature for his age.'

'Ah,' nodded Greg, not entirely in agreement.

'Anyway, let's agree on a routine for him,' Joan moved on.

'Hang on a moment. Isn't it a bit soon for that? I've only taken him out for a couple of times and neither have exactly been a success.'

'Oh, he'll be fine, the more he sees you, the quicker he'll get used to you and you owe it to him to do as much as you can. To make up for lost time.' She was unable to resist that below-the-belt comment.

There was a few moments' silence.

'Who are you again?' asked Ivy.

'Mother, I've told you over and over. This is Simeon's father.'

'I don't think it is. It doesn't look a bit like him, if you ask me. I'm sure he didn't have a beard.'

'Well, it is and we're discussing how he's going to help with Simeon, so please keep quiet. I'm sure he doesn't have much time.'

'Well, actually...'Greg began but then decided against it.

'So my thoughts were that you pick him up from here, take him to school, pick him up and then bring him back here for when I get home, apart from Thursdays when I will pick him up as that's my early finish day. Then you have him on Saturday afternoon. I have something very important then and nothing must upset it.'

Joan gabbled out her well-rehearsed speech and stopped to breathe.

Greg was left floundering. 'That seems quite a lot. I'd been thinking more along the lines of a seeing him once or twice a week.'

Joan shook her head defiantly. 'Without going into details that are no business of yours, you can, by looking around you, get the gist of the problems I am faced with. I want to look after my mother at home for as long as feasibly possible and day care has been a boon, as it means I can go on working as normal. If you help with Simeon, as I suggest, then it will all fit together nicely.'

'How about he goes to breakfast club and after-school club?' suggested Greg, as Rosie had instructed him to.

'No, I'm not keen on those,' she lied and there was no way she was going to tell Greg the truth. 'He's a very sensitive, very bright child who flourishes on a more one-to-one basis. He needs to be stimulated constantly. At those clubs he only messes about and plays. Here, or at your house, he can be encouraged to do his homework and spend less time on frivolities.'

'There's nothing wrong with playing, he's only a young lad.'

Joan ignored this comment.

'It's an awful lot of change for him, all at once,' Greg continued. 'Perhaps we ought to do it more gradually, don't you think?'

'There's no time for that, I mean, it's better we do it this way. You'll cope. You must. He'll cope. He's resilient. He told me how he really enjoyed visiting your house last time.' This was twisting the truth to a considerable degree.

'I need to discuss this with Rosie.'

'No need. I'm sure she'll agree with me. She sounds a sensible enough woman from what I've heard.'

'I can't possibly make decisions like that without consulting her.'

Joan rounded on him, her cheeks flushed. 'Ha! You've changed! You'd never have asked me for my advice and thoughts. Well I'm telling you, you *have* to do this. I mean it. Everything depends on you,' she hissed.

Taken aback, Greg nodded and reluctantly accepted the piece of paper that was thrust into his hands with Joan's instructions in her trademark tiny writing.

'Is there any more tea?' He looked up from reading.

'No.'

He was about to suggest that she might like to be so kind as to put the kettle on but one look at her face was enough to convince him that this was not a good idea.

She dismissed him. 'You can go now. You start tomorrow, picking Simeon up at lunchtime and bringing him back at six.'

Chapter Twenty-two

John was at the kitchen table, head in hands, Faye standing over him waving a chocolate bar wrapper at him.

'What is this?'

'Guilty as charged m'lord,' he confessed. 'I'd missed lunch and was ravenous. It was my first offence, I promise. Be lenient with me.'

'All right. You are forgiven. But only this once. If you stopped to buy this, why didn't you get a sandwich or some fruit instead?'

'Because I saw it and wanted it. But I did feel very remorseful afterwards...'

'As if that makes up for your sins!'

John laughed. 'I know. It really is the only slip-up I've had since I started this diet and I don't intend to let it happen again. Though I can have small amounts of chocolate every now and then, as you know. And you'd hate it if I wasted away altogether... We aren't all lucky enough to have figures like you, darling.'

Faye was in her leggings and tennis skirt, on the verge of leaving for her Saturday afternoon game when she had noticed that the bin needed to be emptied and had come across the aforementioned evidence.

'You old smooth talker, you! Stop trying to change the subject! No, seriously, I'm so proud of how well you've done with your diet and I'm sure this isolated – if that's what it was – indiscretion will have done no harm. Look how much better all your blood tests are. That's the proof of the pudding.'

'An unfortunate choice of words, Faye, if you don't mind me saying, which make me feel hungry. What's for supper?'

'Chicken. We've only finished lunch ten minutes ago. You're impossible! Anyway I must go or I'll be late. Enjoy your afternoon.'

She hurried to put on her coat and pick up her tennis bag.

'Oh, by the way, I hope you haven't forgotten that Joan is coming today, from two until five. I've left a list of things for her to do over there on the worktop. Don't spend the whole time gossiping about work, will you? Can you pay her when she goes please? I've virtually no cash at all. Bye, darling.'

She blew him a kiss.

'Bye! Enjoy your game.'

John spread the newspaper out over the table, refilled his coffee cup and settled down to read. He was planning a lovely, relaxing afternoon, perhaps some sport on television and maybe a snooze if Joan wasn't using the vacuum cleaner too much. Despite the early spring feel outside, he didn't have any inclination to go for a walk and anyway, he'd been on the damned rowing machine that morning for a whole ten minutes without stopping, which was more than enough for anyone of his age.

He wasn't overly enamoured with Faye's idea of offering Joan work. He felt he saw enough of her at the surgery, as a very dedicated employee and frequently attending patient, plus now with the weekly house call to Ivy, which he had to do on his way home so that she was back from the day centre. Yet he knew how more money was needed and he knew that Faye was always one to help if she were able. It was just a shame that Joan was only able to come when he was at home and Faye was out. He wondered if Elliott might be able to free her up during the week and made a mental note to ask.

As if on cue, the doorbell rang and there she was, looking excited.

'Joan,' John was his most ebullient, ever the professional. 'Come on in, my dear. Let me take your coat.'

Joan's trembling fingers struggled with the buttons but finally she succeeded and removed her coat, revealing a tartan skirt and a thin pink blouse with a bow at the neck. The latter was new. She had bought it specially.

'You look too smart to be doing housework,' said John, in a friendly manner. He wasn't used to seeing her out of uniform.

Joan giggled. 'Oh, these old things! Don't you worry! I've had them for years.'

'You've just missed Faye – only by a whisker. Now, where did she say she'd left a list for you? Oh, there it is. The cleaning things are in here…' he opened a door, '…and the vacuum cleaner is in the cupboard under the stairs, along with various other bits and bobs that you might need. As you can tell, I'm no expert. Have a rummage around and see what you can find. Now, shall I show you around the house, so that you know what's where? Or can I leave you to it? We're very grateful to you for your help. Ivy's at day care is she?'

'Leave me to it, please! I'll shout if there are any problems. Yes, I cannot tell you how relieved I was when I heard she was able to go on a Saturday. It gives me some breathing space and some time I can call my own.'

'Hardly your own, coming to clean for me!'

'Oh, that's a pleasure.'

'And Simeon?'

'Would you believe it? By a stroke of luck, his dad got in contact and we all met up and he and Simeon got on like a house on fire from the outset, so he's there with him today.'

John looked taken aback by this sudden progression. 'Goodness me! Well, that must have helped you.'

'Oh, it has. He's remarried and is very happy. I'd hate you to think there was any chance of him and I getting back together.'

'That hadn't occurred to me. Whatever makes you happy, Joan.'

'I'm very happy, Dr Britton, I am. Especially now.'

John thought for a second. 'I think it's only right that when we're outside work, you call me John and Mrs Britton is Faye. Okay?'

Joan fluttered her eyelashes a little. 'Of course…er…John it is! Now,

I must get started or I'll never finish!'

She studied the list, gathered together various cans of polish and cleaner in a bucket, threw in a duster and a cloth for good measure and set off with these in one hand and her large handbag in the other.

'Did you want to leave your bag? You've rather got your hands full,' suggested John. 'It'll be quite safe in the kitchen...'

'No problem. I like to have it with me. It's got my phone in and stuff.'

John shrugged and returned to his paper. The crossword was asking to be done.

Glad to be left to her own devices, Joan decided to start upstairs where her check list invited her to clean the house bathroom and the en suite. Neither was really in any need of cleaning, which was a further testament to Faye's kind heartedness. Determined to set off as she meant to continue, Joan rolled up her slippery pink sleeves and set to. On a glass shelf, she found John's cologne and squirted some onto her handkerchief, for later. Next to it was Faye's expensive perfume, the sort that the likes of her would never be able to afford. There was one nearly empty bottle and one new one, of the same type, still in its Cellophane covering. She jotted down the name in her diary, Moonlight, it might come in useful one day, you never knew.

There really wasn't very much to do at all, which suited Joan perfectly as it meant that there was plenty of time for her to have a good look around. Faye and John's bedroom was spacious. The carpet was cream and mark free, as were the walls, in contrast to the curtains and bed linen which were titian, bronzes and oranges, bringing a warm and intimate feel to the room. John's navy pyjamas, thrown in an untidy pile on the duvet rather ruined the look, so Joan hid them from sight under a pillow, once she had taken her time and folded them neatly.

She felt no awkwardness about opening all the drawers and sifting through the contents. She liked the way they were very clearly either his or hers and was careful not to leave any sign that she had been there. Similarly, she rifled through the cupboards as she dusted around. She found a spare, clean pair of John's pyjamas and after a quick look over her shoulder, popped them in her bag.

John and Faye both had a lot of clothes, though mostly they were Faye's. Again, John (she glowed as she remembered how he had insisted that she use his Christian name) had a wardrobe of his own. It was nice to think that his belongings were separate, suggesting independence and possibly some cracks in their marriage? When she and Greg had been together they had their clothes rammed in any old how but then again, to be fair, they hadn't had any option as space was at a premium.

She vacuumed around, bumping into a few pieces of furniture on purpose, so that it would sound to John downstairs as if she was hard at work. The room looked spotless. Worthy of a photograph. She was sure that Ivy would be interested to see where she was working. There was something wrong though and for a moment, Joan couldn't think what it was. But then she realised and deftly removed all traces of Faye's existence from the dressing table and her pile of books from the bedside table. She closed all the wardrobe doors and moved a few ornaments on the windowsill, which she thought too feminine, behind the curtain. The result was a big improvement. Joan took several photos from different angles before restoring the room to its original state, as near as possible. Were any comments made, well, that was easy, she had moved things to dust. One of the hallmarks of an excellent cleaner.

Silently opening all the other doors on the landing, to have a peep into each room before she came downstairs, Joan was full of admiration for John's home. She had expected to be wowed and she was not let down in any way. Coming here to clean was going to be wonderful. It would bring them so much closer together, give them time to converse properly, not just about the stupid patients at the surgery but to make plans. It was as clear as anything that this time had been chosen for her to be there because it was when Faye was out.

This was no coincidence. It had been planned especially by certain divine influences they were at the mercy of. When she had suggested Saturday afternoons, John had quickly agreed, because he wanted them to be alone, just the two of them.

For the first week, he could act entirely appropriately, as would she as they carried out a charade. She cleaning, he sitting downstairs, pretending to be unaware of each other's existence.

The second week he would begin to drop his guard then all would change and, after brief pleasantries on her arrival, a mutual passion would take over as they both gave into temptation and fell into each other's open arms. Then they would go up to the bedroom and... She had never before felt such an irresistible draw to a man and she instinctively knew the feeling was mutual.

She was shocked out of her day dreaming by John calling up the stairs.

'Do you want a cup of tea, Joan? I'm putting the kettle on.'

'Oh that sounds lovely. I'm on my way!'

He was waiting for her in the kitchen, rolling some water around the teapot to warm it. How she loved his domestication! What a treat it was to have someone wait on her for a change.

'Tea okay, or would you prefer coffee?'

'No, tea is fine. No, no sugar, just milk please. Not too strong.'

'Ah, like I have mine.'

How similar they were in all aspects! Even the most mundane!

'I'll take mine with me and carry on, shall I?' Joan nobly suggested.

'Sit yourself down for ten minutes. There's no rush. I've heard you beavering away up there. You've probably nearly finished all that's on the list, knowing you.'

'Well, I am getting on with things quite well,' agreed Joan, a degree of coquettishness in her voice. 'If I'm honest, it's not exactly hard work. You keep your home very neat and tidy.'

'That's all down to Faye. I'm afraid I'm not really the best at housework.'

Joan forced her lips into a smile before referring to her list. 'I've only the washing to put on and then dust and vac in the lounge.'

John seemed to be paying more attention to his newspaper. Time for some small talk.

'Mrs Britton, I mean Faye, plays a lot of tennis doesn't she?' Joan took a tiny sip of tea. She wanted to make it last as long as possible.

'Yes, she loves the game.'

'When I was computerising the club details, I could see how keen she is. She signs up for all sorts. The winter league, the Dales league. Singles, ladies and mixed doubles. She seems to do everything.'

'She's not so keen on singles nowadays. She says she's not fast enough but I'm sure she is.'

'Are you not a tennis player?'

'Only under sufferance. I don't have the legs for shorts! Seriously though, I cannot deny that it's nice to play on a summer's day but then I always seem to have to serve with the sun in my eyes and so my serves rarely go in. Well, that's my excuse! No, I'm more for watching and the après tennis – you know, the glass of chilled white wine, some egg sandwiches with the crusts cut off and a few English strawberries. I used to like the cakes too but they're banned of course.'

'Why? You've lost so much weight now, surely you can eat what you want.' Joan was outraged.

'It's not simply a matter of losing weight though, Joan. I'm diabetic.'

He surprised himself with this admission. Apart from family and of course his work colleagues, nobody knew. Presumably he had been afraid of telling anyone but for some reason, on this occasion, it had been perfectly easy.

'Oh, I didn't realise. You never mentioned that when I did the interview about your new lifestyle.'

'Why should you? I don't think I've ever told anyone before. I think I might have been a bit ashamed. Perhaps I should've done. It would have sent a far more powerful message to the patients.'

Joan was thinking rapidly. She'd sent him chocolates without being aware that it was forbidden for him to eat them. Whatever would he think? Had he guessed they were from her?

'It doesn't make any difference, though, does it? Being diabetic I mean. We've loads of diabetic patients and they're all out and about being perfectly normal.'

'I am determined that it won't make my life too different. Obviously I need to watch my diet and have regular checks but I'm getting the hang of it now and at the moment all is going well.'

'That's such a relief to hear. You look wonderfully well.'

'Thank you for your concern. More tea?'

'That's so kind, thank you. Half a cup is enough and then I must get on. Still things to do!'

In her wildest imagination, the afternoon could not be going better. He had shared his diagnosis with her. Her! Out of everyone, he had chosen her! Of course Faye knew but she didn't really count.

Humming with happiness, Joan gathered up the dirty laundry from the wicker basket at the top of the stairs and stuffed it into the washing machine. Fondly, she stroked a cardigan of John's, scrunched it up under her nose and inhaled deeply. Remnants of that irresistible cologne clung to the soft, delicate fibres. Such glorious dark green cashmere was obviously not meant to be going in with some shirts, blouses and a pair of size ten jeans (there was no way she wasn't going to look at the label, even though she didn't like what she saw). Joan left the cardigan to one side while she added detergent and, after a bit of head scratching, chose a suitable wash programme. It was a far more complicated machine than hers. On the verge of taking the garment back to the bedroom, it occurred to her that a much better idea was for her to take it home – nobody would notice its absence for a few days – and she could wash it by hand, dry it carefully and bring it back next weekend. Such genius! She folded it carefully and placed it in her capacious handbag, on top of the pyjamas, covering them over with her purse, umbrella and diary so that no one but her knew they were there.

Joan didn't want the afternoon to end. How three hours had flown by. With a feeling of finality, she ventured into the lounge, such a cosy, welcoming room with comfy chairs, two sofas, one of which that was made for two, she noted, and heavy dark burgundy curtains to match the carpet. On a small table under an art deco lamp were three photographs, at the front, two of the family and behind them one of John and Faye, maybe taken when they were on holiday, but standing very close to each other, looking so happy. She hid it with the cardigan, hatching a plan as she did of what she intended to do with it.

A quick vacuum around and she was done. Though part of her desperately wanted to eke out her visit for as long as possible, she wanted to be away before Faye returned more. She knew that even a glimpse of Faye would ruin everything. Anyway, doubtless Simeon would be on his way back for tea and the hospital transport would be bringing Ivy back soon. It might be rather nice to celebrate a little and have fish and chips for supper. Maybe not. Simeon would only eat the chips and the batter and Ivy would worry about bones. Pizza was so much easier and anyway, she was too excited to eat. Ivy liked soup, so that was her taken care of as well. Hopefully she'd have had a proper lunch at day care, though in all probability, she wouldn't remember.

'I'm done now!' she called, while she put away all the cleaning equipment, arranging them as she liked them, rather than as they had been.

'Joan,' John marched into the room, arms outstretched. 'What a great job you've done! So grateful to you. Now let me settle up with you. You must be desperate to get home and have some well-earned time off. Any plans for this evening?'

He found his wallet in his back pocket and took out a couple of notes. 'There we are. And cheap at the price, if I may say so. Faye will be thrilled. Same time next week?'

'I've so enjoyed being here,' gushed Joan. 'It really hasn't seemed like work at all and it's so very lovely to spend some time with you, getting to know you away from work. The money will be so helpful. I can't wait until next Saturday. You can give me much more to do. I can cope you know.'

'I'm sure you're as capable at cleaning as you are at being a receptionist. Now, where did I put your coat?'

He ventured out into the hall and returned with the said garment, holding it up for her so that she could slip it on. Joan leant back a little as she let her arms drop down the sleeves and felt the pressure of his chest on her back. Best of all, he didn't recoil, but then she had known beforehand that he wouldn't. What a perfect end to a perfect afternoon!

Chapter Twenty-three

Unexpectedly, Joan found she had a whole afternoon to herself. Elizabeth owed her half a day and Elliott suggested she took it sooner rather than later when it might be lost in the mists of time. Reluctantly, for she was quite convinced that nobody was either able or appropriate to look after Dr Britton in her absence, she agreed, partly because she did feel tired and her work at home was piling up at a rather alarming rate, partly because she had the next edition of *The Teviotdale Telegraph* to finish off and had a very important article to write for it but mainly because Dr Britton had promised her that he would manage for an afternoon and she deserved a bit of free time. It was his way of paying her a compliment. The underlying message his words conveyed only the two of them understood. Such shared secrets were delicious. She knew he had to be careful about such things, especially at work.

She was finding, not surprisingly, that by the time she had fed Ivy and Simeon and coaxed the two of them into their beds, she had little or actually no enthusiasm for housework or ironing. All she felt capable of was sitting down with a cup of tea, a couple of plain biscuits and the television. Since hearing about John's diabetes, she had carefully read up about the condition, securing some patient information leaflets from the practice nurses saying that they were for a friend, recently diagnosed. Having pored over these while sitting in bed, she was now an expert on the day-to-day life of a diabetic and knew by heart what foods were good and which were not. Accordingly, she had adjusted her own diet. It was only fair after all. How cruel it would be to sit and eat one meal while your other half had to have something else? So the chocolate and sweets had gone from the cupboards, the cake supply was minimal (Ivy was particularly partial to a slab of cherry Madeira – when angel cake wasn't available – and couldn't be denied that) and the fridge secreted no cans of fizzy pop.

Initially, Simeon had not been amused and had made his feelings known in no uncertain terms. But, to Joan's amazement, after a few days, he had stopped making a fuss, had been eating his meals and then heading off to his bedroom to do his homework. Without being asked, which was remarkable in its own right. Some might have been suspicious at this change in behaviour but Joan was simply thankful. He did seem to have an awfully large amount of homework, she thought briefly.

It was Simeon's room that Joan decided to make a start in that afternoon. With a sinking heart, she opened the door and went in, grimacing at how much disorder she was faced with in such a tiny space. It didn't just look appalling, it smelled pretty awful as well.

Picking up an armful of clothes that were strewn around the floor, she began to try to create some order from the chaos. Separating the clean from dirty garments, the former were folded and put away, the latter thrown onto the landing to be dealt with later. Now at least she was able to see the carpet and once the duvet was straightened and the pillows placed nicely and smoothed over, there were definite signs of improvement. A cereal bowl, age of contents unknown, was peeping out from under the bed. Joan bent down and rescued it, half stood up and then sensibly had the thought that there might be more where that had come from.

Narrowly avoiding kneeling on a stray piece of Lego, Joan lifted up the valance and peered into the dark recess. To her surprise, it was crammed full of objects. This needed further investigation. It was totally alien to Simeon to put things away, even if it was just shoving them out of sight. Joan scoured around the room and found what she was looking for – Simeon's torch. Miraculously, not only was it switched off but it still had batteries which worked.

Returning to the bed she shone the feeble beam underneath and not without some trepidation began to pull one or two things out of the way so she could see what else was there. Before long, in a heap in front of her, were bars of chocolate, a cake, bags of crisps, cans of pop, video games she had never heard of and didn't like the look of, what looked like a brand-new mobile phone and tablet and a new games console.

What? How? The answer came to her immediately.

Greg!

How could he? Had he more money than sense? Trying to buy Simeon's affection in this way? Had he no idea of how to forge a relationship with the boy? Had he been put up to this by the oh-so perfect Rosie? Wasn't she supposed to be a teacher for goodness' sake?

Joan was livid. Incandescent with rage, her normally pale face suffused with anger. No wonder Simeon had stopped creating at meal times. No wonder he had been so keen to go and do his homework. Homework! Not a chance in hell had he been doing any studying. He'd been stuffing his face, watching vile videos and playing bloodthirsty games. She pushed everything back under the bed and then marched down to the lounge and angrily punched out Greg's number on her phone.

Simeon came home from school on time, nonchalantly took off his coat, throwing it in the vague direction of a hook and shouted to his mother that he was off to his room as he had a lot of homework to do and so should not be disturbed. Joan counted to ten, until she heard his bedroom door close, counted a further ten to compose herself and then bounded up the stairs and burst into his room. He looked up guiltily from the chocolate he was eating.

'Where did you get that from?'

His eyes darted from side to side before he triumphantly came out with, 'Um, Dad gave it to me.'

'Did he now?'

'Yes. He's very kind. Rosie gave me some too!'

Joan put her hands on her hips.

'Really? How lovely for you? Why the need to hide it under your bed?'

'Because you're trying to make us eat healthy food all the time. And I love chocolate. And it would be wrong not to accept presents from Dad, wouldn't it?'

Joan pushed him to one side and crunched onto her knees, pulling out, one by one, the videos, tablet, phone and sweets.

'What about all this? Where did all this come from?'

'Dad.' Simeon shook his head apologetically. 'He told me not to tell you. So I hid them all. He's always giving me things. He's very rich. Don't be cross with him, please.'

Back on her feet, Joan sat on the edge of the bed, tossing the handful of videos she had onto the floor after uttering disgusted noises as she read the title of each one. She looked up at Simeon's quasi-angelic face.

She smiled. 'Of course I'm not cross with your dad. I'm so pleased you're getting on so well. Isn't he generous?'

'Yes, I'm so lucky.'

Joan looked at him, studying him – from his scuffed shoes, grubby grey trousers (the recently bought ones – nearly ruined already) to his shirt hanging out and jumper in disarray. He stared back defiantly and stuffed a piece of chocolate into his mouth.

Joan took in a deep breath. 'Simeon! How could you! You're lying, I know you are. I know your dad didn't buy you these things. I've spoken to him! He knows nothing about them. So where did you get them from? Look at this,' she picked up the phone, 'this is a latest version. It will have cost hundreds of pounds. Did you steal it?'

'No, I never,' he replied.

'Stop lying. You're in enough trouble as it is, without making it even worse for yourself.'

There was an awkward hiatus.

'Go on, I'm waiting...'

Simeon had never seen his mother so angry. Usually he could soft soap her round, crying a little always helped melt her heart and before long she would be trying to hug him better and apologising for her behaviour. Today there was something definitely very different about her and he knew that his normal tactics were going to prove totally impotent. Worse still was that his grandmother was not there to act as his immediate and reliable ally.

'I'm waiting...' Joan increased the menace in her voice by a couple of notches.

'I bought them.'

Joan spluttered. 'Don't make me laugh! You bought them?'

'Yes. Really.'

'That's ridiculous. They cost the earth, some of those things. Wherever did you get money like that?'

'I saved up?' Simeon tried helplessly.

'Stop wasting my time. I know that you've never been able to save money. So let's start again. Where did you get the money?'

'From Granny.'

'Okay, so she gives you money for sweets and perhaps a bit extra for a new game. But there's no way she's going to give you hundreds of pounds. Please tell me you've not been stealing from her handbag.'

'We...ee...ll, she didn't exactly give it to me. I'm sure she would if I asked but nowadays you can't have a proper conversation with her.'

'How many times do I have to tell you? She's ill, Simeon. She doesn't understand like she used to. So how did you get it?'

Ashamedly, Simeon pulled open the pirate chest at the bottom of his bed, extracted an elephant that used to be a pyjama case and unzipped it. He pulled out Ivy's credit card and handed it over to his mother.

Joan was appalled. Lying was bad enough. Stealing was a different ball game altogether. His behaviour shouted a total lack of respect for his grandmother who adored him. He had coldly calculated that she would be oblivious to his actions now that her dementia was so much worse.

'How dare you!'

Joan was shaking now from head to toe, struggling to suppress a tremendous urge to hit out at her son. By now, even Simeon had acquired an unusual pallor.

'How did you get her PIN?'

'She asked me to get her some money one day. We'd walked and she wasn't feeling well and wanted to sit down.'

'Tell me it now. I'm going to the bank to get it changed so that you can never do this again.'

Why oh why had she not taken the good Dr Helliwell's advice and sought a Lasting Power of Attorney while Ivy was able to understand what she was signing? Joan knew the answer. She had simply been too preoccupied with work and home and the subject had completely been forgotten about. However much had Simeon stolen? There was a pile of post addressed to Ivy in the lounge, waiting for Joan to go through but that was yet another job she had never got around to. She had a nasty premonition that reading Ivy's bank statements was not going to be pleasant.

As soon as she had dropped Simeon off at school the next morning, Joan made a beeline for the bank. She had barely slept for thinking about what had happened. It was unspeakable. The lack of sleep had resulted in a most hideous headache, like cymbals having a fight. Half way through the night, it had occurred to her that the bank were not going to give her another PIN just like that however much she begged and pleaded. But at least she had secured the card so that Simeon was unable to use it any more to satisfy his own greed. He really was an evil child. It was hard to credit that she had given birth to him. It wasn't that rare to read about the wrong baby being brought home from the hospital. Maybe that's what had happened to her. Okay, bringing him up had been a struggle but she'd done a good job, she thought. Certainly, she didn't deserve this outcome. Once he had gone to bed the previous evening, she had rung Greg again and ranted so loudly down the telephone with barely a pause for breath and included a veiled threat that she might lash out, that Greg had promised to take their son for the whole weekend, so that Joan could calm down.

As the night had progressed and she had made a mental list about going to a solicitor to discuss a Court of Protection order, going back to Dr Britton to discuss her headaches and how she must come up with a suitable punishment for Simeon, something else had occurred to her of far, far greater interest and as soon as it dawned on her, she wondered why ever she hadn't thought of this earlier.

The bank might be closed but the ATM outside was available and waiting with no queue. It was no more than borrowing really, was it? Just to tide her over until she had everyone's finances sorted. The outlook in that respect was definitely more encouraging than it had been for a long time. Joan was confident that when Greg became closer to his son, then he would be making a regular payment towards his upkeep and they would all be significantly better off. Plus there were other significant changes in the offing, of these Joan had no doubt and while they were on the cusp of change, had she been in a position to be asked then, without a doubt, Ivy would have bent over backwards to help.

She inserted the card, punched in the PIN and without the merest hint of compunction, extracted two hundred pounds. That was a good start.

Chapter Twenty-four

What made him make the final decision, John, if asked, would not have known the answer. After months of ruminating and prevaricating, he simply woke up one morning and knew. It wasn't a particularly dreary morning weather-wise, nor was it one of those fabulous starts to a day that radiate optimism. He had slept well the night before. He felt fit and happy and for once had no really difficult problems with patients that were worrying away at him.

No, he simply woke up and decided that today was the day to announce his retirement. In six months. There was to be a partners' meeting at lunchtime and that would be the perfect time to say what his plans were as they'd all be together, which was how it ought to be.

He whistled in the shower. What a good feeling it is when you know instinctively that something is right. He dressed with care, choosing his favourite yellow shirt, a rather racy green bow tie, slid his newly sylph-like body into brown corduroy trousers and nodded with approval at his reflection in the mirror. To complete his outfit, he needed his dark green jumper. Now where was it? Checking the wardrobe yielded nothing as did looking through the chest of drawers. How odd! The laundry basket was empty, Faye having done a wash the day before. Presumably his jumper was hanging up drying somewhere. He shrugged and found a red V-neck instead.

Thinking no more about it, he ate his porridge and toast with the feeling that a weight had been removed from his shoulders. Faye received the news ecstatically. Of course, they had discussed his retirement innumerable times and she had sensibly sat back waiting for him to come to the final conclusion. She gave him a huge hug.

'I'm delighted, darling. Well done. I know it's not been easy for you. You're so committed to your career but I've seen you become so unhappy over the last few years.'

'I feel it's the right time for me to go. Quit while I'm ahead. Well, I think I'm just about still ahead.'

'Of course you are. Let's start making some exciting plans so we've lots to look forward to. Give me a ring after you've told the others. And try not to be late. I think I might make a celebration dinner.'

To the partners, the news was bittersweet. They all knew it was coming and their reaction was one of elation for John and sadness at the thought of him going. Elliott greeted the news with equanimity and made a note to put an advert in the *British Medical Journal* for a new partner as soon as possible, ever the efficient manager. Quietly though, he was very gloomy. He and John had a unique bond when it came to running the practice, a mix of professional and personal that suited them both. It was going to be hard to have the same with Ellie, a very different personality, who by virtue of seniority was about to become senior partner, much as he liked and respected her.

'When are we making the news common knowledge?' asked Ed.

'With immediate effect, I think,' mused Elliott. 'We all know how rumours spread. It's better that we're up front with the staff and anyway, when the advert goes in for a new partner, all the world will know. Is that all right with you, John?'

'Of course.'

'Right. This afternoon, I'll email everyone here. We need to get cracking. Six months will pass before we know it. Anyone know of someone looking for a partnership? Ed? Any registrars finishing their training this summer and wanting to stay in the area?'

Much muttering from the others ensued about the sort of person they wanted, ideally.

Suddenly John felt marginalised. It was as though he wasn't there, as though he had already gone. Like a ghost he was hovering over the meeting, wondering how he would cope without work, which for so long had probably been his raison d'etre. He so wanted to contribute his ideas about the sort of partner he thought they ought to be looking for but it had nothing to do with him and he forced himself to bite his tongue and stay quiet. Was he making the right decision?

Elliott's email caused a flurry of excitement in reception, as can be imagined. Much whispering passed between Gary, Gemma and Elizabeth, with furtive glances over their shoulders to make sure than Joan wasn't about to pounce and berate them for their behaviour. The telephones were definitely left to ring for longer than they usually were and Miss Chisholm had to bang on the counter with her fist to get some attention.

As it happened, Joan hadn't even noticed the slight slipping of standards. She was far too wrapped up in herself to care one jot about her colleagues. John, retiring! It was a sign! For her! Soon they would be able to be together. How perfectly this was all working out.

All week she had been crossing the minutes off until Saturday afternoon, willing time to speed up. She might arrive a little early as she was sure that he would want to discuss it all with her then. She felt both nervous and excited about going round to John's, suspecting that little cleaning would be done. Since last week she had laundered his jumper with the greatest of care ready to take with her. One day she would let slip how she had worn the jumper in bed, loving the feel of it touching her skin when she knew that it was his. How flattered he would be. How they would laugh as they talked about all the tiny but significant events that slotted into place and led up to them being together.

The pyjamas she planned to keep a bit longer. They looked so right on the pillow beside her own.

How much better that photograph looked, the one she had 'borrowed', now that Joan had carefully cut Faye out and inserted one of herself. She kept it by her bed; it was very special after all and every time she looked at it, as she settled down to sleep, Joan would imagine about the day it was taken; her favourite fantasy being how she and John had been having a glorious day out in the Yorkshire Dales, strolling hand in hand, having a delicious pub meal and then they had stopped a stranger to ask them to take the photo as a lasting memory.

How odd that they had worked together for years but only recently felt the force of attraction to each other. Or had it, in actual fact, been going on for a lot longer? She remembered her very first day at the medical centre, how she had been introduced to all the doctors who were there then and how Dr Britton had seemed aloof and a little frightening. Obviously he must have known, that very day, from the moment he set eyes on her, that their destiny was to be entwined but had shied away and put on an abrupt, professional facade. What a fabulous performance he had continued to act, fighting his feelings for her, waiting for the right moment to admit that he loved her. Joan knew that he wasn't happy with Faye. She could tell. She was so in tune with him that just a glance at his face spoke volumes to her. His looks of concern, ostensibly because he was worried about a patient, his staying at the medical centre for lunch when he only lived a stone's throw away and his loneliness as Faye repeatedly left him to go and play tennis.

Maybe she too had loved him since they met, her feelings gently simmering beneath the surface ready to boil over in the last few months, which had been so memorable. It didn't really matter. The ripening of their love was like a huge jigsaw and slowly but surely, the picture was taking shape and soon the final piece would be put in place.

The day dawned overcast but fine. Joan felt anxious. It was imperative that it stayed like this as rain might mean that Faye abandoned her tennis and chose to stay at home in the dry, putting on the pretence of being a good wife. Over the course of the morning, she repeatedly referred to the weather forecast on the television or gazed out of the windows, making her own assessments. A slight shower mid morning had her stomach churning with worry but it was brief, if heavy. Thank goodness for all-weather tennis courts.

To be honest, it was a blessed relief not to have Simeon there. Both she and Ivy were more relaxed and you could almost hear the house itself breathe a sigh of relief. He had gone to Greg's after school on the Friday, under sufferance but probably very relieved to be away from a seething mother who spat venomous menaces every time she saw him. Her anger had not evaporated as the days had passed.

As for Ivy, well she'd gone off to day care, asking if it was nearly Christmas. The staff there were simply marvellous with her and all the other clients. Their patience was seemingly endless.

Luckily, Ivy loved it. She had a bath there, it was a huge one in which you could lie and soak for as long as you wanted. She had her hair done and sometimes her nails as well. The chiropodist saw her every few weeks and although she had been quite hesitant to start with, she now even enjoyed the massage and aromatherapy sessions. She adored the food, the musical entertainment and the general fussing over that she received.

So while Ivy was enjoying a hearty lunch, for Joan, eating was not an option. Her excitement was spiralling out of control, her gullet a row of knots, past which nothing was allowed to pass. Breathing deeply as an aid to calm, she showered, took care over dressing, finally deciding on a camel-coloured turtle-necked jumper, a dark green tweed skirt, which she had thought in the shop looked quite 'countrified' and some smart shoes in dark brown leather – a bit like brogues but with higher than her normal heels. Another similarity to John. They both favoured the same colours!

She had so enjoyed her shopping trip earlier in the week. It had been so exciting not to have to pay attention to the price tag, even if it had meant taking a bit more money out of her mother's account but as she 'borrowed' more, the qualms she felt about doing had become fewer and fewer. Joan had no intention of using all the money. Only enough for the most important items, those she felt were vital.

Pleased with the result, she brushed her hair and applied a modest amount of makeup, attempting to emulate a look that she had seen in a magazine. It had worked wonders for a Mrs Phillips of Weybridge who had won a makeover in a competition. Perhaps it didn't quite work out the same for Joan but the end result was still flattering to her mind and she was sure than John would appreciate the effort she had gone to.

Finally, it was time to go. She squirted some of her new perfume on her pulse points, tried on a necklace of green beads but then removed it, carefully stowed the jumper away in her bag, did a quick twirl with excitement and headed for the car, ignoring the sound of the telephone which started to ring as she stepped over the threshold.

Chapter Twenty-five

Faye and John were in the bedroom, getting ready. Faye put down the receiver.

'There's no reply, she must have already set off.'

'That's a shame. We could have saved her a journey,' replied John, choosing which tie to wear.

'I can't turn her away at the door. She's expecting three hours' work and some money for doing it.'

'Just give her the money then.'

'She'd never accept it. You know what she's like.'

'Well, how we were to know that Helen and Angus were going to ring last night and invite us out for the afternoon and dinner?'

'We weren't. We knew they were coming over this way sometime soon. Anyway, it doesn't matter. It'll be so lovely to see them and it's great that they're going to come back here and spend the night. There you go, that's something for Joan to do – get the room ready. It's still in a state from when my brother stayed the night before last. I still can't get over him forgetting his pyjamas and asking to borrow yours!'

'Ha,' John laughed. 'He's always forgetting something. I was sure I had two spare pairs but I could only find one. Not that it matters. Does this tie look okay?'

Faye inspected him and shook her head. 'No, change it for the lovely blue one I gave you.' She stopped in her tracks as the doorbell chimes echoed around the house.

'Lawks, here she is! I'll go as I'm ready. Be quick, darling. We don't want to be late.'

She ran down to the hall and unlocked the door.

'Oh Joan, I tried to ring you but you must have set off!'

Joan's face must have dropped considerably when the door was opened by Faye, who, to make matters worse, was not in her tennis clothes. She was looking glamorous in a knee-length black dress with white collar and cuffs and some high heels that looked very expensive. Perhaps she changed at the club though she didn't exactly look like someone who was about to get hot and sweaty. This was not in the script that she had prepared.

'Come in anyway and let me explain. What lovely perfume you've got on. I think that's the same as mine. Moonlight, it's called. What good taste we both have! Beautifully light and flowery isn't it?'

Joan was glad of Faye's chattering on as she was still trying to recover from the shock of an entirely different greeting to the one she had been building up in her mind. Where was John?

Covering up her confusion by rummaging in her bag, she mumbled, 'Hello, Faye, no tennis this afternoon? Or are you playing later?'

Never give up hope.

'I wish! No, we've had a last-minute invitation to meet up with some very good friends we don't see often. They live in Canada and are back on a flying visit. I was going to tell you not to bother coming today.'

'It's no trouble. I'm here now. I can still do my work and then let myself out when I've finished.'

'Are you sure?'

'Absolutely. Let me know what you'd like doing. I promise to stay my full shift and not leave early.'

'I don't doubt you for a moment, Joan. Do you mind ironing?'

'Not at all.'

'Well, if you could just vacuum around, have a clean up here in the kitchen and then the ironing basket is in the utility room. I've been washing curtains this week, so there's a pile that needs pressing and leaving to air. Oh, and can you change the sheets on the bed in the spare room please. The clean linen is folded on the bed waiting.'

'Leave it to me. I'll do a really good job.'

Faye laughed gratefully. There was something incredibly earnest about the expression on Joan's face.

'I'm sure you will. Don't worry if you don't get through it all. Now do make cups of tea and coffee as you need them, won't you? You know where the biscuit tin is? Where is John? We ought to be leaving... John!'

Joan heard him coming down the stairs, smelled his cologne before he came into the room and when she caught sight of him, her insides performed somersaults of delight. In a dark blue suit, he looked the epitome of handsomeness to her. He must have had his hair cut that morning. A bit drastic for Joan's liking but it would soon grow.

Their eyes met, very briefly but easily long enough for her to know what he was trying to tell her. He was apologising for this disruption of their time together, telling her how he didn't want to go, how he would rather be with her and that as soon as he could, he would make it up to her.

'Hello, Joan. All well with you?' he asked, almost brusquely, tugging at his tie which he felt was strangling him.

'Yes, thanks. You're looking very smart if I may say so.'

'Yes, doesn't he scrub up well?' Faye interrupted.

Joan forced a smile, not liking the rather common expression that Faye was using. It was verging on derogatory, suggesting that under normal circumstances, he looked a mess. Poor John. He deserved so much better. She was never going to treat him like that. She watched them leave and heard the car engine start. In the past five minutes, her joy and excitement had been stamped out like an unwanted firework.

Before she had a chance to turn and decide what to do first, the door opened again and in rushed a frazzled-looking John.

'I had to come back,' he said.

Joan was unable to breathe. Her mouth went dry. Was this going to be the moment?

'Forgot my coat!' he gasped. 'It's perishing out there. Blooming friends not giving us any notice! Oh it's on the chair behind you. Excuse me, please.'

Gently he put his hands on her shoulders and steered her to one side as she appeared to be rooted to the spot, watching him. Joan's entire body felt as though it had been brought alive by electricity running through it. Although his touch lasted no more than a second, he had branded the imprint of his fingers on her skin and she could still feel it, scorching through her shoulders, even as he disappeared from sight when the door closed behind him.

It wasn't that cold outside. She had only worn a thin jacket. Spring was definitely in the air. The coat was simply an excuse to come back in for them to have a few precious moments together, moments that promised that there was so much more to come.

Her disappointment vanished, she set about her work with a bounce in her step and after no more than a cursory spell with the vacuum cleaner, spent a far more satisfying time peeping in cupboards and rifling through drawers, trying to find out as much as she could about John. She sat in what looked like his chair in the lounge with her coffee, but no biscuits. She found some old photograph albums and studied each page in detail, absorbing the change that had taken place in John over the years. He had obviously been a great family man, according to these pictures but then she knew that already from the ones in his consulting room. What was of much greater interest to Joan was that she spotted that almost exclusively the photographs included either John, or Faye. Rarely were the couple together with their children. The rational explanation that one or other of them had been the photographer never occurred to her. No, there was a deeper meaning. The cracks in the marriage had been starting many years ago. They had stayed under the same roof for the children's sake.

Upstairs, she ventured into the spare room where John's fitness equipment was. A rather nasty, damp tee shirt was hanging over the handlebars of the bicycle, suggesting that he had been using the machine earlier that day. The duvet was in an untidy pile, a couple of paperbacks hidden amongst the folds and Joan made short work of stripping the bed down, until she paused because, surely, these were John's pyjamas. She had seen them and hugged them last week. What was going on?

She knew. Instinctively, she knew. John was starting his preparations to leave Faye. He had moved out of the marital bed and into the spare room. There was no other conclusion. Evidence a-plenty supported her theory. The fitness equipment was in this room, so were his pyjamas and the signs that someone had been sleeping in the bed were unmistakable. She needed to make him aware that she had seen this and understood, that she approved and was supporting him all the way, waiting for him patiently for that moment that was becoming ever closer. Once the bed was made and tidy, a job she carried out with considerably more care than she had apportioned to the vacuum cleaning, she dashed down to her bag in the kitchen and found John's jumper. She would leave this in a secret place for him to find. Under his pillows, she thought. When he realised it was there, he might want to sleep in it, as she had done.

Chapter Twenty-six

Elliott was sitting at his desk, sleeves rolled up to his elbows, three mugs in front of him, two of which were empty, looking at the end-of-month statistics for the practice. This was not his favourite task as he was usually able to predict with incredible accuracy what the figures would show. However, his job was to perform these rituals regularly and diligently and so he had set about this as soon as he had arrived at the practice at his customary hour of seven o'clock in the morning. Not surprisingly he was always first in these days. Before Clare had become a mother, it had been her habit to come in excruciatingly early and have a good, uninterrupted hour or more of solid work before the floodgates were opened.

The number of available appointments was more or less set in stone, so no change there. There had been a slightly larger use of the emergency appointments, for which an outbreak of an influenza-like illness was probably responsible. The doctors had all seen the usual number of patients, though why Dr Britton had had a drop in numbers was obscure. He had had no holiday or absences on educational courses to account for this discrepancy. Elliott checked the figures again and came out with the same result.

Odd.

He shrugged, took a gulp of cold coffee and moved on.

Drs Britton and Diamond were good time-keepers by and large, Ellie and Faith had their moments for running horrendously late and, of course, Clare was streets ahead when it came to how long patients had to wait between their arrival and when they were seen. He doubted that he could make any change to that and, anyway, Clare's patients adored her so much that they rarely, if ever, complained about the wait.

He was well aware how, over the years since she had first joined, John had repeatedly discussed her consulting technique with her, trying his best to help. She had even taken videos of her consultations and then the two of them had watched them back, trying to spot areas where perhaps she could speed up but though John was able to spot room for improvement, Clare could not. Her constant riposte was that when the patient closed the door behind them, she had to feel that she had helped to the very best of her ability. Anything less than this and she would not have been able to go home and relax. Motherhood, John had predicted, would lessen her intensity but the change was minimal, if at all. She needed to learn how to let go and leave work behind sometimes but all the signs pointed to her never being able to do so. Clare would feel bereft without John's support but no doubt the others would take over, especially Ellie, to whom she was very close.

Elliott was on the verge of moving on to look at house-call figures when he spotted something anomalous. The number of appointments where the patient had failed to attend was remarkably high for the practice. Almost four times the usual number. Thinking back, he remembered that this had been the case the previous month but he had attributed it solely to a hiccup from the norm and forgotten all about it. What on earth was going on? Their patients were doggedly devoted to the doctors.

A search showed him that the non-attenders were nearly all booked with Dr Britton. Several, every day. This was more than a blip; this was curious to say the least. Bit between his teeth, Elliott probed in more depth, looking to see which receptionists had booked these particular appointments. With the exception of one, they had all been booked by Joan. Was this relevant? He really didn't know what to make of this. Joan was a reliable, hard-working woman, for whom he had never had any concerns or worries. On the contrary, she was the one he felt he could leave to get on with the job and know that all would be well.

He scribbled some notes to come back to and examined the house calls over the last month. Again, about the expected number had been requested. But, again, there was an inconsistency. Why had Dr Britton done so few in comparison to the others? On quick inspection, it looked as though patients hadn't been requesting him to call which was downright bizarre. Some questions needed to be asked. Elliott looked at the clock and realised that morning surgeries were drawing to a close. He emailed John, asking him to pop in for a moment as soon as possible.

'What do you make of these?' Elliott handed John a piece of papers covered with numbers. 'Have a look while I check something further quickly.'

John sat down and cleared a space for his mug of coffee on Elliott's desk, trying to avoid anything that looked vaguely important. He read the information, aware that Elliott was tapping his front teeth with the end of his pen as he did so.

'Odd, aren't they?'

John nodded. 'I've definitely been aware of lots of non-attenders but I always have so many other things to be getting on with that I haven't added them up, or questioned them. But as you're asking, it is odd. A lot of the patients in this list usually see one of the other partners and I remember Ellie commenting that this pair here,' he pointed, 'weren't even in the country or so she thought. I've rung through to reception more than a few times and offered to help the others out – you know, have some of their patients transferred to me – but I'm always told that there's no need and everyone is managing fine.'

'By whom?' asked Elliott.

'Any of them really, though to be fair, it's usually Joan I speak to.'

Elliott pondered for a few minutes. 'Everything seems to point back to Joan, for a reason I've yet to work out. While you were reading, I did another search on all those non-attenders and without exception there is no log of any of them having telephoned in. Which makes a further nonsense of the whole business. Have you any concerns about her, John?'

'She's normally a really reliable receptionist and I think she loves the job. I guess my only comment would be that she's trying to burn the candle at both ends and maybe she's worn out. You and I both know that she has huge problems at home, what with her mother and that boy of hers and money is always an issue for her. So much so that she's doing a few hours cleaning for us on a Saturday, which strictly speaking ought to be a day off for her.'

Elliott nodded. 'She certainly has a lot on her plate. I'll need to have a word with her and get her view point though doubtless she'll say that there's nothing wrong.'

'Well, from what you've told me, something's awry. That's a weird way to behave at work.'

'You've done all right out of it,' Elliott laughed. 'Look how much time she's freed up for you.'

John replied with a sardonic smirk. 'I think I'll have a word with her too.'

'Maybe best if you let me do it first and let you know what she says.'

'Okey dokey,' agreed John. 'Well, I'd better be off on my visits. Time marches on.'

'Hang on,' Elliott raised an arm and with his other hand clicked on the screen. 'There, I rest my case, you have no requests for visits today. Again.'

'Well, I'm off to find some. I'm not having anyone saying that I'm not pulling my weight as I approach my retirement.'

Chapter Twenty-seven

John was still wondering about what Elliott had shared with him when he started afternoon surgery and noticed, not without some misgivings, that Joan was booked into the last appointment. He wasn't sure if he felt ready to tackle her yet; aware that he wanted to give more thought to the situation than he had had time to do so far. His plan was to talk it through with Faye; his thoughts characteristically fell into a better order when he did this, plus there was the added bonus of her common-sense views, as an outsider. He had gone home for lunch to do this but she was out shopping, so though the opportunity to confront Joan was there for the taking, he was going to leave it until another day.

It had turned very cold and the skies were heavy with possible snow, so before returning to work, he had put on his dark green jumper, which had reappeared as mysteriously as it had disappeared when Angus had found it on going to bed. For some reason it was making him itch. He wondered if Faye had changed the washing powder but knew that she would not have done, aware of his sensitive skin.

He also found that he was not looking forward to seeing Joan as inevitably she was going to want to discuss her headaches. For several months now he had reviewed her on a four-weekly basis, asked innumerable questions, repeatedly examined her (she had this thing about having the backs of her eyes looked at and always asked him to check very carefully and thoroughly) and found nothing untoward and tried everything he could think of that might help but nothing had. Initially he had been quite optimistic about the tablets he prescribed, having had huge success with them in other patients but now he had a sneaking feeling that he was only prescribing to bring the consultation to an end. In desperation, he had offered to refer her to a neurologist on several further occasions but, each time, she emphatically answered no.

She seemed increasingly hesitant about leaving his room. His instinct told him that this was because there was something important she wanted to let him know, something that she was afraid to talk about, most likely the key to the whole problem. He tried all the tricks of his trade that he knew. He asked his partners for their advice and tried their suggestions.

All to no avail.

'Perhaps she's got a crush on you,' offered Ellie, only to be met by a withering look from John.

'What utter tosh!' he responded.

His visits to Ivy were fortuitous as they gave him plenty of background information and he was adamant that her headaches were stress related, which was perfectly comprehensible and acceptable. Indeed he had nothing but sympathy for her predicament. Joan, however, was reluctant to accept this diagnosis. Yes, there were difficulties in her life but she did not think that they were to such an extent that they were having any sort of impact.

John made a valiant attempt to prolong all his earlier appointments. If his patients were surprised at the rather unexpected extra questions he was asking them, they did not show it. Try as he might, probably due to the fact that three patients did not turn up, he ran to time and his cunning plan of finishing so late that he suggested to Joan that he saw her another day (aware that she would be in a rush to get home for Ivy) was foiled. He ambled to the door to call Joan in.

She bounced in, glowing. Not exactly the entrance for someone in chronic pain, he thought. On the contrary, she looked exceedingly well. That might be a new hairstyle but he was hopeless at noticing such things, as Faye would corroborate. He smiled a well-trained smile.

'Joan! Come on in and have a seat.'

She did as she was told, pulling the chair a little closer to him as she settled. She spotted the green jumper instantly and knew he had worn it especially for her.

John clasped his hands together and placed them on the desk. 'So, how are things? You're looking great.'

The corners of her mouth turned down and her shoulders slumped. 'No better. I'm so sorry. I've tried so hard with the new tablets but the side effects were quite awful. They made me very dry mouthed and constipated and of course that would never do with my job and looking after my mother and Simeon. I had to stop them.'

'Yes, of course.'

She looked at him, head slightly tilted, waiting for his next move. He sat back in his chair, hands now behind his neck. The itch was making it impossible to get comfortable.

It was so tempting to rush off yet another prescription and go for the quick finish and although it was difficult to put a finger on it, there was definitely something a bit different about her.

Was she really being flirtatious or was it his imagination? What rubbish, he thought, deciding the only way forward was to do things by the book.

'Okay. These headaches are a real puzzle. Let's start at the beginning. Describe them to me.'

With a fine-toothed comb, he made her go through everything and, if he wasn't mistaken, she relished the opportunity. The descriptions of her symptoms were nothing short of flamboyant. It was a thankless task, not helped by the itching on his back and he learned nothing new.

He examined her, stopping to cough when he got nearer to look into her eyes. Her perfume was very strong. It smelled familiar but he couldn't think where he'd come across it before. As usual, there were no abnormal findings. Clearing his throat, he prepared to start reassuring her.

'There is one other thing, Dr Britton,' she interrupted.

'And what's that?' Maybe at last this might be the clue he needed.

'I keep getting palpitations. I can feel my heart racing. I wonder if you'd have a quick listen. I'm sure it's nothing but it's happening a few times a week, not for long.'

Dutifully, John asked more questions, which unsurprisingly did not help. He checked her pulse which was regular if a little rapid and reached for his stethoscope. Without being asked, she undid all the buttons on her shirt. The top three would have sufficed.

A woman might have noticed that her red brassiere with the black frills was verging on the provocative and had doubtless been very expensive but such minutiae were lost on John, who had examined so many female chests over the years that he never paid any attention to such things.

'That all seems fine. From what you've told me, I think this is most likely stress and the first bit of advice I'd give you is to cut caffeine out, completely. Eight cups of coffee a day is a lot. You've never mentioned that before and I've lost count of how many times I've asked you, thinking it may play a role in the headaches. Another idea is, how about I see if I can get some respite care for Ivy for, say a fortnight. That'd give you a real break, wouldn't it?'

'Oh, there's no need for that. I'm managing fine at home. Thank you for your advice, as always. I'll try the coffee approach first. Decaff doesn't taste the same, does it? But I'll really give it a go.'

'I'm sure you'll feel a lot better and the palpitations will stop. If they don't then we can arrange an ecg and some bloods but there's no need to rush into that. With any luck, the headaches will be better too. Just a point though, when you stop the caffeine you may get some rebound headaches for a couple of days while it works its way out of your system.'

Joan oozed gratitude, sitting on the edge of her seat and leaning towards him as she buttoned up her blouse rather slowly. As she tucked it into her skirt, she deliberately thrust her chest towards him. She felt jubilant, dominant. Her very presence was unnerving him. He was constantly shifting about in his chair, fighting against the temptation of wanting, no needing, to take her in his arms. She knew he had loved her new underwear. In the fullness of time, he would find out that there was plenty more where that came from. He was such a consummate professional, keeping his feelings in check like this but at the same time letting her know that the time was getting closer and closer when they would merge as one.

So lost in her daydream, Joan didn't hear a word of what John was saying, closing the consultation in no uncertain terms and it was only when he got up and went to open the door, that she giggled and jumped up.

Going back to his desk to write his notes, he viciously pulled off his jumper and threw it onto the examination couch. Instant relief!

Chapter Twenty-eight

Saturday morning and Joan had her hands full, getting Ivy up and dressed while Simeon caterwauled downstairs, wanting his breakfast instantly, impatient to go and play outside as it had snowed heavily overnight.

Joan was not similarly excited by the weather. She was fretting and oblivious to the beauty of the view from the windows. The customary untidiness of the road they lived on was disguised by several inches of perfect whiteness. Even the discarded tricycle in next door's garden had acquired a sort of beauty.

Listening to the forecast on the radio, there was more to come, intermittently for the next few days. Never mind that, it was today that was her major concern. All she kept thinking was that the transport for Ivy might not be able to get to the house and pick her up.

Nothing was allowed to ruin her day, which she knew was going to be one of huge importance.

Ivy seemed rather more wobbly than usual. Probably she's cold, Joan diagnosed, helping her into thick grey tights over which she pulled woolly trousers and then socks. She added another pair of socks for good measure. Better too much than too little. A shirt, jumper, quilted waistcoat and cardigan completed her outfit. Nothing really matched. Ragbag she may resemble but at least she would not be cold. They made their uncertain way down to the kitchen where Ivy was safely delivered to her place at the table and awarded some breakfast.

The telephone rang and Joan was the recipient of the terrible news that the day centre would not be opening that day because of the awful weather. Nearly all the staff had rung in to say that they were snowed in and the slippery paths were decidedly unsafe for anyone, let alone those of unsure footing. Hopefully, normality would be resumed on Monday. They were very sorry for the inconvenience but there was nothing anyone was able to do. Platitudes about the British weather had no ameliorating effect on Joan.

Incipient panic coursed through her body. This wasn't allowed to happen. She had other plans of far greater importance. It was imperative that she went to John's that afternoon. He was expecting her and Faye was away for the weekend. He had vouchsafed this vital snippet of information yesterday afternoon, when she went in with some late prescriptions to be signed.

Away for the whole weekend. Kismet was calling them.

Joan's mind was a maelstrom of thoughts as she tried desperately to come up with a solution. Her eyes darted from side to side in the hopes that something, somewhere might provide a clue. The pounding of her heart in her chest made her breaths come in short, sharp gasps and her fingers began to tingle.

A blast of cold air swept through the kitchen as Simeon bounded out into the little back garden, forgetting to close the door after himself. Joan shut it hurriedly, disregarding the fact that her son was still in his pyjamas and slippers and looked at Ivy, who hadn't touched her toast and marmalade, preferring to nod off to sleep, despite having only been up for less than an hour.

Then, a brainwave.

Relief swept over Joan like a warm shower as she remembered that Greg was coming to pick up Simeon. Well, the weather was too horrible to go out anywhere, neatly providing the perfect answer. So she would suggest that they stay in the house until she got back, though this might be late, keeping an eye on Ivy at the same time. It wasn't a hard job. Ivy in all probability would be fast asleep during her entire absence. Phew! Problem solved. Some unknown deity was smiling on her that morning!

She set about her morning tasks, singing as she did so. Activities such as dusting and organising the washing rarely filled her with any sort of excitement but today she was simply bubbling, like newly poured champagne and nothing was going to make her otherwise. She had been awake most of the night before but in a happy, expectant way, planning what she was going to wear, what she was going to take with her, what she was going to say and thrillingly what he was going to reply. Lack of sleep had not dented her exhilaration, on the contrary, she was high with anticipation. Who needed drugs to create this feeling? Love was a far stronger stimulant than any chemical one.

It was nearly time for Greg to arrive. She rather liked the thought of the intrigue she was going to create when he saw her dressed and looking her most glamorous. A red dress, daringly low cut at the front with its scooped neckline, sleeves to just below the elbow (very flattering for the more mature female arm) and slim fitting over her hips. Normally a dress like this would not have got a second glance on its hanger but the personal shopper who had taken her round (for a hefty sum of money) had insisted that the colour suited her perfectly and that there weren't many women of her age who had the figure to carry off such a style, once she had bought the necessary underwear. Joan had blinked when she saw the price but, with a trembling hand, she handed over a handful of crisp notes without any second thoughts.

In the future, she was perfectly willing to think that she and John might see Greg and Rosie socially. She could picture the four of them, dining out, somewhere eclectic. Why not? It was inevitable really, with Simeon being the common denominator. But only if John wanted. There was no way that anything was to upset him. It was going to be difficult when he and Faye first split up. Their friends would take sides, there would be criticisms aplenty, some more cruel than others but when everyone saw how happy John was, a totally new, splendiferous dimension of his life having been opened up, then they would understand and celebrate the new couple.

Joan wished Faye no harm. She saw her more as a rather inconvenient blot on her horizon, which needed to be removed. Faye was an attractive woman. Male suitors would flock to her, once they heard that she was on the market and Joan wished her nothing but the best for the future, so long as it was not with her husband John. Anyway, maybe she was already embroiled in an affair with one of the male tennis players! Who knew!

She cursed when the telephone rang again. There was no time for interruptions when she was about to start on her makeup.

'I'm sorry,' said a voice she instantly recognised. 'There's no way I'm going to make it over today. We've nearly four inches of snow here.'

Joan was appalled. 'But you have to, Greg! You've got a big car. It'll be fine and I'm sure the main roads will have been cleared by now.'

'Well, our main roads might have been but the side roads certainly haven't and it's far too treacherous to take the car out. It'd be bloody stupid even to try. I'm not risking an accident or getting stuck.'

'Simeon!' shrieked Joan, becoming hysterical. 'What about him? He's so looking forward to seeing you. You can't let him down. He's built a snowman in the garden for you.'

'I'll have a word with him. He'll understand and he can send me a photo with that new phone of his.'

'No, no, no!' By this time she was screaming. 'This won't do. You promised to have him every Saturday. Look, come over here and stay here for the afternoon. Stay overnight if you like. Bring Rosie! Bring the dog! You have to come! I have an appointment I cannot miss!' She would break the news to him about Ivy once he was here.

Joan was far too distressed to hear the exasperation in Greg's voice.

'Joan, look outside. Be reasonable. It's simple. I'll not be over today. It's starting to snow again as I'm talking. Heavily as well. I've said

I'm sorry but surely you can understand. It's not exactly quantum physics. Whatever your appointment is, I bet they're expecting you to cancel. Now then, let me speak to the lad, please.'

'I think it's beginning to thaw here.' It was her last, frantic attempt.

'The temperature's below zero. Are you all right? You sound hysterical. It's only one bloody afternoon. Get a grip!'

'Fine, fine. You are as useless as ever! I hope for your sake that Simeon isn't too upset. You'll have to live with this on your conscience. He's gone very pale. I think he's crying. Simeon! Dry your eyes, darling, and come and speak to your horrid father.'

Leaving father and a completely unperturbed son to chat, Joan sat down and put her head in her hands. Her dreams were on the point of being shattered. This afternoon was such a god-sent opportunity. She chewed on her newly done nails and then stopped as she didn't want to spoil them. There must be something she could do.

Slowly, through the fog, an idea came to her and its simplicity made her laugh out loud. The answer was there in front of her and she felt foolish for not having thought of it sooner. It was so obvious!

'Simeon?' she called.

'What?'

'Have you finished on the phone?'

'Yes.'

'Come here then. I have to go out this afternoon. I want you to stay here and look after Granny. Okay? It is very important that you do this.'

Simeon scrutinised her with suspicion. 'What's in it for me?'

Joan rolled her eyes but today she was not going to argue. She grasped at straws.

'I'll pay you.'

'How much?'

'Ten pounds?'

'Make it twenty.'

'What?'

CHAPTER TWENTY-EIGHT

'Well, remember I'm so upset because I'm not seeing Dad.'

'Fine.'

'What if she wants to go to the toilet? She always wants to go to the toilet and you know she doesn't like me helping her and I don't like helping her either.'

Joan thought rapidly. 'Tell you what, let's put her in bed and give her one of her sleeping tablets and then she'll snooze all the time I'm away and be no trouble to you at all. You just stay down here and watch TV but keep an ear out in case she calls for you. You've got my mobile number, so you can ring me if you're worried. I'm sure it'll all be fine though. How about that?'

Simeon nodded his agreement, only half listening... He had a new game that he'd bullied someone at school into letting him borrow and he was longing to give it a try. Well aware that his mother would not approve one iota about its content, this was a stroke of luck as far as he was concerned.

Chapter Twenty-nine

What Joan had failed to include in her elaborate equation was that it wasn't just the day- centre minibus and Greg who felt that the road conditions were too bad for travel. Faye, too, had decided that it was madness even to set off and see how she got on and so she had rung to cancel her indoor tennis weekend. This had turned out to be a serendipitous move as John had come home from surgery, feeling diabolical and, having succumbed to some sort of virus, he had taken himself off to bed, where he lay feverish and miserable after a bad night coughing and spluttering.

Having dosed her patient up with paracetamol and honey and hot lemon, Faye was surveying the kitchen cupboards with a view to a long overdue thorough clean out. She had tried to ring Joan but her number was continually engaged. Anyway, the likelihood of her turning up in this weather was remote. So, with a fresh cup of coffee close by, Faye opened and proceeded to empty the first cupboard, determined to declutter with ruthlessness.

Joan set off and made her way precariously down the crescent. Underfoot was treacherous, even with wellington boots on as she had. She almost lost her balance on a couple of occasions. Children keener than Simeon had been out with their sledges at first light, compacting the snow and exaggerating its slipperiness. The main roads, she was pleased to find, were considerably clearer than she had expected and she was lucky enough to find a taxi, the driver of which agreed to take her to the end of the lane that John lived on, but no further. He drove at an excruciatingly slow pace. Joan wanted to scream and take the wheel. Any old fool could see that the road was safe to speed up on.

Eventually, she was deposited at her destination and she attempted to hurry to John's house, knowing that he would be anxious for her safety. His drive had not been cleared, so Joan had to wait until she was on the doorstep to change into her high-heeled shoes.

Faye jumped out of her skin when the bell rang. For a moment she had no idea who it could be. The postman had triumphed against the elements more than an hour ago and the delivery they were expecting had been postponed until Monday.

'Good gracious!' she exclaimed on opening the door and finding Joan, who was stamping her feet in the cold. 'It never occurred to me that you would venture out on a day like this. Come on into the warm and defrost. You must be freezing.'

Joan was revolted by the sight of Faye, looking infuriatingly slim in jeans and shirt as she followed her through the house. Initially she was unable to speak, her mind working overtime as to why her plan had gone wrong and was there any way in which she might be able to salvage parts of it.

'The main roads are quite passable,' she gulped, glad that she was looking at Faye's back as there was no way she would have been able to muster a smile.

'You never drove here, did you?' Faye was aghast and turned to her.

'No, I got a taxi and walked the last little bit.'

'In those shoes?'

Joan looked at her feet as if she had forgotten what she was wearing. She half laughed. 'I've left my boots on the doorstep. I didn't want to bring any slush in.'

'You're always so thoughtful, Joan. And dedicated. I can't get over you being here. I've got a coffee I've only made a few minutes ago, let me make you one. Have a seat by the radiator and get warmed up.'

Joan did as she was told. The shock was receding, anger rapidly taking its place. She was shaking a little but sat up straight, adopting a rather aggressive pose. 'I thought you were away for the weekend.'

Faye glanced over from the kettle. 'I was but I watched the forecast yesterday and didn't want to risk it. I so hate driving in the snow, don't you? Years ago I got stuck once after I skidded across the road. I was all on my own and found it really frightening, so I wasn't prepared to take any unnecessary chances.'

'Oh. What a shame you didn't go.'

Faye took this reply at face value, not realising its true meaning. 'I know but we'll rearrange and go another time. Here's your drink. Have some ginger cake. It is homemade but sadly not by me. A friend, who is a great cook, gave it to me. I think it's delicious. John has never been a fan of ginger so isn't keen.'

Joan made a show of crumbling the piece of cake, nibbling a little and then leaving the rest, which was hard for it was indeed very good. 'Sorry, ginger's not for me either,' she lied.

Faye cut a large slice for herself. 'Anyway, it's a jolly good job I am here as poor John is upstairs in bed, ill. I'm blitzing these cupboards, as you can see, so when you're finished we'll crack on with that. It'll be nice – we can chat at the same time, can't we? You can tell me all the secrets of the surgery!'

Joan felt that the very last thing she wanted to do was 'chat'. 'What's wrong with John?' she enquired anxiously. 'Nothing serious, I hope.'

'The usual stuff. High temperature, sore throat, cough. Doubtless a gift from one of his patients.'

'Oh the poor thing. Can I do anything? Take him anything? A drink perhaps?'

'Thank you but he's fine at the moment and probably asleep. I'll check on him in a short while. You know what it's like when you're ill. You just want to sleep and sleep and be left alone. But, you can put money on him being back in surgery on Monday as usual. What's he like? He admitted that he was ill on Friday but didn't like to come home – which he should've done – for fear of letting the others down. They're all the same, the partners, never look after themselves, carry on regardless when really they'd be better taking some time off.'

Joan got up and took her mug to the sink. Small talk such as this made her uncomfortable. Better to get on with the job and work out a way she might have a glimpse of John.

Between them they were making short work of the cupboard clearing. Secretly amazed by some of the unusual ingredients she came across – what on earth was galangal of all things? – Joan's focus was on speed. She was virtually monosyllabic with her replies to all of Faye's attempts to chat, trying hard to disguise the curtness in her tone. She did not want to hear about the Brittons' friends, family, holidays, parties and the mere mention of the word tennis made her want to vomit.

Somehow an hour passed. Faye nipped upstairs, leaving Joan to polish some crystal wine glasses, and found her husband sitting up in bed, looking washed out but better than he had earlier.

'Who are you talking to?' he asked. 'I can hear you chattering away.'

'Joan. She turned up in the snow, looking all glamorous. What on earth made her bother to take even one step out of her house today baffles me. She knows we'd have understood.'

'Well, keep her away from me. I need to rest. I'm not fit to receive visitors...' He pulled a face.

'Of course. I'm going to tell her to go early before it gets really icy. She's a good worker, you can't take that away from her. She's done a splendid job in the kitchen, even if I don't know whether I'll ever find anything again! Now then, how about a drink? What do you fancy? And something to eat?'

'Hot blackcurrant sounds good to me. Funny how I hate the stuff when I'm well but when I'm like this, it's delicious. Even though the sugar-free version isn't a patch on the real stuff.'

'Anything to eat?'

'Not now, darling. Thanks but what I'll do is get up when Joan's gone and come down and maybe have some soup and toast.'

'Perfect. Good to hear you're feeling ready for something solid.'

She leant over and kissed him on the cheek. 'I hate it when you're poorly. Be up in a mo with that blackcurrant.'

'I'd prefer a proper kiss.' He puckered up his lips.

'Not a chance until you're better!' she joked.

He blew her a kiss as she left the room, rested his head back on the pillows and closed his eyes. He felt absolutely drained.

'He's asking for a hot drink,' Faye told Joan, who grabbed the kettle and rushed to the sink.

'How is he?'

'He looks a little better now, poor soul. Don't look so worried! I'm sure it's only a humdinger of a cold. He's never been a good patient. So I'll take that up to him, you just finish off those last glasses and then go home. It's been so good of you to come but I want to think of you warm and snug at home with your mum and Simeon. I'm sorry I can't or rather daren't offer you a lift but I'll call a taxi for you though I expect you'll have to do as you did earlier and have them pick you up on the main road.'

Joan was starting to panic. Time was slipping through her fingers at an uncontrollable rate. She *had* to see John. Even the briefest of peeps was needed to keep her going through the rest of the weekend. How to orchestrate this – that was the question. Fate owed her a favour or two she reckoned after the let-down of the afternoon.

Faye filled up the mug with hot water and had reached the kitchen door when miraculously the shrill ring of the telephone gave Joan the chance that she required.

'Drat,' said Faye, putting the mug down on the table and walking to the phone. 'Oh hi, Jo! How are you? Yes, isn't it a shame… No, of course I've time to chat.' She sat down on the window seat.

It's now or never, thought Joan. Faye is obviously going to be a while. She felt as though her heart might burst through her ribcage as, in an instant, she snatched up the mug, gesticulated to Faye that she was going upstairs, ignored the instructions not to bother (it would be easy to say that she had interpreted Faye's arm waving as being given the go ahead) and bolted up the stairs, paying no heed to the amount that was spilt on the way. No one would notice.

She tapped gently on the bedroom door and tiptoed in. John was asleep, mouth wide open and dropping to one side, but even such an inelegant position filled Joan with lust. For a couple of moments, she stood still and watched, synchronising her breathing with his, which was hard as she was about to start hyperventilating with pleasure. Time was not on her side, she knew that, she needed to act quickly. Drink safely delivered to the bedside table, she carefully and slowly sat on the edge of the bed and patted his hand.

'Thanks, darling,' John mumbled, not really waking up but putting his hand on top of hers. 'I do love you.'

The words she had longed to hear and uttered when he was ill too! Emboldened by these, Joan leant forward and kissed him first on the forehead and then, ever so gently, on his lips.

He smiled. 'I knew you'd see the error of your ways.'

Much as she wanted to stay, she knew she had to leave. Faye's footsteps were audible on the stairs, getting closer and closer. She backed out of the room, making the most of her last seconds in his presence.

'There was no need for you to have done that,' Faye stopped her on the landing. 'I was only going to be a minute.'

Joan put her finger to her lips. 'Shhhh, he's asleep. I've left the drink in case he wakes in the next few minutes while it's still hot. Now, as you've advised, I'll ring for that taxi and get off home.'

Outside it was dark and huge snowflakes were tumbling down. Faye was concerned to see her leave but Joan knew that enough was enough. Though the afternoon had not turned out as she expected, there had been an undeniable magic to it. Nothing could burst that balloon. Not even the recalcitrant taxi driver who grumbled at having had to come out of town to pick her up when really all he wanted was to be in his own home watching the football results, not even Ivy who was lying soaking wet in bed and had also had an accident with her bowels and not even Simeon, who, high on artificial additives and sugar, had undone all the housework that she had done that morning.

Chapter Thirty

Contrary to forecasts, the snow disappeared with its customary speed, much to the delight of adults and the disappointment of children. Easter was fast approaching, being very early that year, bringing with it indisputable signs that spring was waiting around the corner.

John was amazed at how time was speeding past and his retirement was coming ever closer, a prospect which he viewed with mixed feelings but mostly those of relief. His patients had been hugely supportive of his announcement. They had read all the scary stories in the papers and heard the perpetual arguments on television and the radio. They knew how stressed doctors were and what a parlous state the National Health Service was in. Of course they would miss him – he had been such a wonderful doctor and friend and nobody would quite be able to replace him but they understood his need to go. John was humbled by their reactions. A small part of him had, for some reason, expected them to be cross as if they considered that he was giving up on them. Only Miss Chisholm had voiced her displeasure at his leaving.

'You promised not to retire until after I'd died,' she grumbled over and over again, upping the number of her visits to see him so that she could make the most of him while he was there.

A few leaving cards had even started arriving, somewhat prematurely to be fair. The words he read were touching beyond belief and as for gifts, he was already the lucky recipient of a case of wine, a gardening book and a pair of slippers. Clearly his patients had their own ideas about what he would be doing with his newly found spare time.

There had been a rather miserable response to the advert for a new partner, yet another sign of the current climate in general practice and it had taken Elliott no time at all to sift through the applications, come to the conclusion that there were no suitable candidates and file them all in the bin. He had re-advertised, spreading his net more widely and hoped for a better response and there was fast becoming a sense of urgency.

With the finishing line in sight, John found that coming to work was less arduous and his mood lifted consequently. He and Faye were having a wonderful time planning what they were going to do in the Autumn, when he was free and the summer tennis league was over, the number one choice to date being a trip to Canada, somewhere they had both wanted to go for many years, though this was very closely followed by getting puppy, a black Labrador, maybe two if he could persuade Faye. Animals had always been a big part of their lives. Only recently had they been without any at all and they agreed that the house seemed empty without the ruckus of large paws, wagging tails and smiling, faithful brown eyes. Amongst many other benefits, they would give John a reason to walk regularly, something he felt no urge to do when he was alone or with Faye but add in a dog to the equation and the whole experience was lifted to a new and preferable level.

He was imagining choosing two puppies (he knew Faye would give in once she saw them) and wondering what would be suitable names, as he sauntered into his consulting room to start work.

To his surprise, on his desk, there was a large, no that is the wrong word, a veritable behemoth of an Easter Egg. Its elaborate decoration of white and yellow flowers, lambs and rabbits was no doubt a work of art but the sight of so much chocolate made even him feel sick. What the¾?

Who had bought this? Was it another leaving gift?

A label was protruding from the yellow ribbon which stretched around its girth. John carefully picked it out. All it said was 'suitable for diabetics'. No other clues.

He rang through to reception.

'Good morning, John, I mean Dr Britton,' Joan responded promptly, raising her voice so the others heard her use of his Christian name. 'How can I help?'

'Have you seen this enormous Easter egg? Where has it come from?'

'Oh, Dr Britton, it was dropped off last thing, yesterday. I was putting my coat on so I didn't see who left it. Gary says he thinks it might be the same person who left you that lovely Christmas present but he doesn't know their name. I've told him off for not paying more attention. Sorry not to be more help.'

'I wish I knew who it was. It must have cost a fortune.'

'Then someone thinks very highly of you. You enjoy it.'

John replaced the receiver, thinking. It was all very mysterious. He still had no idea who the cheese and wine was from. Nobody had owned up to being his benefactor during consultations in or out of the surgery and he had felt sure that they would have. But his first patient was knocking on the door and it was time to focus on the day's work and revisit this puzzle at a later date. So with a sigh, he turned his attention to the much more important matter of Mr Wottle's ongoing prostate problems.

Joan was busy with a telephone call when a message popped up on her screen from Elliott, asking her to come into his office at her earliest convenience. Something told her that this did not bode well. She sent a message back saying that it was chaos in reception and could this wait but received the one word answer of 'no'. Fluffing up her recently newly styled hair and slipping her feet into her high-heeled sandals, which she now wore daily at work but took off at every opportunity as they really were quite painful, she instructed Elizabeth and Gary that she would be with Elliott should they need her and not to hesitate to call if they were struggling before making her way across the waiting area and up the stairs to Elliott's office. His door was ajar and he was waiting for her, sitting behind his desk, flicking through some paperwork and gnawing on the end of a pencil. She tapped softly and he waved her in, barely looking up.

'Sit down,' he instructed.

She did as she was told, crossed her legs and put her hands together in her lap, meekly. It was vital that she kept her cool.

He put down his pen and gave her his full attention. 'Ah, Joan. Thanks for bobbing in. Sorry you're all having such a bad morning.'

'Oh, it's not that bad. I just don't like to leave Gary and Elizabeth on their own for too long. They do have a habit of getting into a bit of a pickle...'

'Really? I thought they were excellent and reliable. Especially Gary, who has really turned up trumps for us. The patients love having a male receptionist.'

'Yes, yes,' agreed Joan hurriedly, 'he's been a good addition to the team. I confess I was doubtful when he started but as you say, he's proved his worth.'

'Indeed. Still, I haven't brought you in here to talk about them. I want to talk about you.'

'Me?'

'Yes, you.'

Joan smiled her best smile, coupled with some wide-eyed innocence. 'Why would you want to talk to me? Have I done something wrong?'

Elliott sat back in his chair and looked at her. 'You're behaving differently. I've always thought of you as one of the most conscientious members of staff we've ever had but lately, I've begun to notice that maybe you're not performing to the best of your ability.'

She swallowed hard. 'Oh my goodness! In what way?'

'Part of my job is to audit all the information about appointments each month. How many have been made, who has made them, whether they're kept or not. Also, all telephone calls to the medical centre are logged, every day. I know that you have been booking people in to see Dr Britton when they haven't contacted the surgery.'

Joan simpered. 'Well, that'll be the people who come to the desk to make their appointments and don't phone. We have lots of those every day.'

Elliott shook his head emphatically. 'But then these patients don't turn up to see Dr Britton. One or two I could understand, but it's becoming ridiculously frequent. Dr Britton has noticed, so have the others. And then there's the house-call requests...'

'I...er...I,' Joan was stumbling over her words.

'And it doesn't end there, does it? Look at the newsletter.' He picked up the last six copies and waved them at her. 'You started off doing this so well. Everyone, without exception, was impressed. The doctors loved it and the patients seemed to also. It was a great idea thinking of doing an interview with various staff members but you've now done six articles on Dr Britton and none about anyone else. And what's this bit – one of Dr Britton's favourite recipes? And this – knit yourself a cardigan like Dr Britton? What is it about Dr Britton?'

Joan's brain had gone into overdrive. She had to hold it together for just a little bit longer. 'I can explain,' she began, slowly, taking her time despite her urge to rush, preferably out of the room.

Elliott cocked his head to one side. 'I'm waiting,' he said.

'Well, it's like this,' she started earnestly, looking to either side as though checking to see if anyone else was listening, 'I've been so worried about him, Dr Britton, I mean. Being the receptionist responsible for him, I've seen him more closely than anyone else and, well, he's been so tired and stressed, trying to work so hard. I'm not a doctor but I've been concerned that he might be depressed. I had a friend once who was very depressed so I've read up about it. He reminds me of her. So I thought that if I gave him a bit more time to do his work in then that would help ease his burden and it seemed to easy to do it without anyone noticing. As for the newsletter, lots of patients put in requests for more information about him in my suggestion box. And I believed it might be good for his self-esteem to see how popular he is. Or so I thought...'

Elliott raised his eyebrows and was about to speak but Joan hadn't finished.

'I'm so so sorry. I realise I was wrong to do it. But I'm so busy trying to help everyone that I don't know if I'm coming or going, what with my mother – she gets worse every day, Simeon, the return of his father into our lives and then worrying about Dr Britton. Oh, it's all a bit too much for me. It's getting out of hand!'

Joan covered her face with her hands and began to make sobbing noises.

'Joan, Joan, why didn't you come and discuss all this with me?' demanded Elliott but not in a harsh way. 'You could have saved so much trouble.'

He was not a hard man, despite the military precision with which he ran the practice and the slightly scary aura he was able to emit.

The sobs continued in between which Joan blurted out, barely lifting her head.

'I thought I could cope. I didn't want to bother anyone. I didn't want to get Dr Britton into trouble. I was afraid I'd lose my job and I must be bringing money in to keep going. Please don't sack me. I won't do it again. Please, please.' She fumbled in a pocket and found a large handkerchief.

Elliott shifted uncomfortably in his seat. Weeping women had never been his strong point. 'Look, try to stop crying, please. The last thing we want to do is lose you. But you've got to start behaving in your usual efficient manner and leave the worrying about Dr Britton to me. That is, if there is anything to worry about. I promise you I will check. Perhaps you should swap and look after one of the other doctors inst¾' He wasn't allowed to finish.

'No, no. Definitely not. We're all very happy with this arrangement and apart from my silliness, it's working well, isn't it?'

Elliott conceded that indeed it was.

'See,' Joan told him. 'There's no need to make that change is there?' She blew her nose loudly.

Shaking his head, Elliott gathered up a handful of papers. 'I'll give you three months' trial. I shall be monitoring all the work you do on the computer regularly so I shall know immediately if there are any aberrations. All right?'

Sobbing afresh, Joan tried to express her huge gratitude. 'Thank you so much. I won't let you down. I can see the error of my ways. How foolish I've been. I'm an idiot, putting my job in jeopardy like this. I know that now.'

Weeping, she stood up and made for the door, her face covered with her handkerchief. Before leaving, she peeped over the edge of it.

'Don't worry, Joan, I'm sure it'll all be okay. I shall be bringing this matter up though at the partners' meeting next week. It's only appropriate that I do. Now wipe your eyes and then get back to work as soon as possible.'

She nodded subserviently and scuttled to the ladies' toilet where she leant on the washbasin and gazed at her reflection, breathing deeply. The look in her eyes was almost feral. There was no sign of her having been crying. Elliott was laughable to be taken in by a performance like that. She was rather impressed by how she had handled him. It had been easier than she had expected, wriggling out of that one but the downside was that now she also knew that the partners were going to be made aware of what she had been doing in a few days.

It was almost perfect timing. She couldn't have asked for better. She needed an incentive such as this to push her into bringing everything to a magnificent climax and her new plan was almost finalised in her head. But time was not on her side and she knew she had to act fast.

Chapter Thirty-one

It was all floating together effortlessly. Her worries about how to manipulate certain events into a preferred sequence had been a waste of time as with an uncanny precision, Fate had dealt her one lucky strike after another.

Never mind the telling-off from Elliott, all that would fade into insignificance by this time next week, or sooner. He had no idea of what was about to happen. Why should he? He was always so busy running the medical centre like some stupid military manoeuvre that he had tunnel vision and was oblivious to anything going on around him. What a shock he was going to get!

People like Elliot prided themselves on being able to deal with anything that life could throw at him but this revelation was going to floor him! Joan rather wished she could be a fly on the wall when everybody heard about her and John. For sure it would ricochet round the medical centre like a bouncing ball. How hysterically funny it would be to hear their reactions and see their astonishment!

And they were going to find out very soon...

Tomorrow John would be coming, as was his habit, to visit Ivy on his way home from work. His visits were typically workmanlike and fairly brief and Joan could not help but admire his restraint when they were in the room together. How hard it was to resist when their auras were being magnetically drawn to each other? The reluctance in his voice was clear for all to hear as he declined tea or coffee or something stronger. But tomorrow was going to be different. He had told her that he had something he wanted to discuss and though he had added that it was about Ivy, Joan knew that this was a ruse. She had seen that look in his eyes and the way he had smiled as he had told her gave the game away.

So everything had to be perfect. She had a lot to do. First, she needed to be her most assertive.

Simeon did not take the news kindly when he was told that his father would be picking him up from school and taking him back to his house where he would stay the night.

'Why?' he asked in a whiny voice.

'Because I'm telling you.'

'That's no reason. He makes me do my homework and go to bed early.'

'That sounds very sensible to me.'

'And they make me sit at the table to eat my tea.'

'Quite right.'

'And they don't let me have sweets, well not many.'

'Excellent.'

'But...'

Joan was having none of his protestations. 'You'll enjoy it. You know you always do.'

Simeon sneered. 'As if... I don't know where you've got that idea from.'

'Well you're going and that's an end to this discussion.'

'You're horrid. You just get worse. I hate you.' He marched out of the room and clomped into the distance. She heard him kicking the commode as he passed it.

Joan, victorious, ignored him, turning on the television and searching for a weather forecast to check that there was no snow promised which might scupper her plans this time. She was relieved to find that a nondescript day was promised, though from her point of view it was going to be anything but.

After a much better sleep than she expected, Joan woke, energised. She threw on her work blouse and skirt before bustling Ivy out of bed, into her clothes and downstairs in record time, intermittently shouting at Simeon who she knew was wide awake and simply hiding under his duvet, pretending that he couldn't hear her. Under normal circumstances, this would drive her mad and she would end up angry and issuing threats of various sanctions but his antics bounced off her that morning; she was impervious to his attempts to procrastinate.

As soon as she had waved Ivy off in the day-centre bus, Simeon was marched smartly down the road to school with a jam sandwich in one hand and a box of juice in the other, both of which he threw into a neighbour's garden. Joan ignored him. Never mind the fact that he had not had any breakfast because he had been messing around, Joan strongly and quite rightly suspected that there were crisps and sweets in his school bag, rather than books. It was a silent journey and neither of them felt obliged to kiss the other goodbye. Not that this was a habit either of them enjoyed at the best of times.

Now her time was her own and back at home, Joan did something unheard of and rang in sick, pleading the worst headache ever and needing to sleep. No, she was really sorry, she couldn't hang on and speak to Elliott, she felt far too ill, so please would Gary just convey the message and she promised she would ring in that afternoon and let them know about tomorrow. No need for him to contact her. She was off to bed to rest.

As she expected, Elliott rang back about ten minutes later.

'I'm so sorry,' Joan apologised putting on a weak voice. 'It's come on out of the blue. I rarely get headaches like this and it's a corker. I know from experience that all I can do is surrender to it and lie in a darkened room...no, no I don't need to see a doctor...yes, I'll be fine...thank you for your concern...of course...yes, I'll ring you later...goodbye.'

Her heart was thumping; that was another hurdle she had overcome. With each successive bound, her excitement and anticipation grew exponentially. She forced herself to calm down and sit with a cup of tea and a half a slice of toast – any more than that would have been too much. Her stomach was writhing and gurgling and seemed to have a life of its own. Better to keep going and channel this surplus energy to good use. She had made a list of what needed to be done and there was plenty on it to keep her busy and assuage her nerves. She tossed her work clothes into the laundry basket with a flourish of triumph. There was every possibility that they would never be worn again in her new life, which was about to start. She had no doubt whatsoever that her days as a receptionist would be over when she was with John. He wouldn't want her to carry on with such lowly work or indeed work at all in all probability.

Dressed in some casual trousers and a baggy sweater, neither of which did her any favours, not that it mattered because nobody was going to see her, she set about cleaning the house as best she could from top to bottom, bar Simeon's room as she would simply close the door and hide all the mess inside.

Adrenaline driven, the housework proved to be an easy task and she flew through the rooms, plumping up cushions, dusting, vacuuming and polishing. She wished she had a more attractive house to welcome John into. His house was stunning. His kitchen made hers look like a glorified cupboard and his lounge – well – imagine the parties that they would be able to hold in there. How easy was it to imagine her as a sparkling hostess, in her element with a tray of homemade canapés in one hand, the other hand resting on John's arm or shoulder, showing everyone what a perfect couple they made. Garden parties in the summer, sauntering on the lawn in a flowing, flowery dress, serving champagne and strawberries! Christmas in the future, golden and red, twinkling lights inside and out, a huge tree, presents and good food. No expense spared and definitely no need for mistletoe. The last thing they were going to need was any excuse to avoid tactility and be open about their love for each other. Like a press-stud, they would match perfectly and cling together for always.

The very thought took her breath away. She was trembling visibly and kept dropping her duster. After a while she realised she was using a pair of Simeon's pants that she had picked up off the landing floor.

Now the house was ready, she was to focus on herself.

Though it was only late morning, she poured herself a small glass of sherry and knocked it back in one, shuddering as it shot down her throat, leaving a trail of fiery heat as an aftershock. It did the trick though and, feeling decidedly calmer, she put on her coat, picked up her bag and scurried to the hairdresser as the first part of her personal preparation.

Needless to say, this was not her usual hairdresser who was used to cutting and blow-drying her hair into the same bob she had had for years. No, she now patronized the newish beauty treatment rooms in the next town (Lambdale had yet to move with the times and acquire one of these), where, for an eye-watering sum of money (thanks to Ivy) she had recently discovered low lights and a more flattering style, which, if the hairdresser was to be believed, took years off her and made her look decidedly girlish.

She left, flawlessly coiffed, a couple of hours later, in a haze of cough-inducing hairspray and ammoniacal odours, shoulders back, head held high, feeling wonderful but almost afraid to walk in case she spoiled anything. She lingered for a while and did a little shopping, wanting everyone to turn their heads and look at her.

Back at home, she began the preparations for dinner. Ivy always had a good lunch at the day centre so would be perfectly happy toying with a sandwich, which gave Joan plenty of time to concentrate on the real meal. She was planning to serve, for her and John, melon with Parma ham to start with, nice and simple. The last thing she needed was to be spending loads of time in the kitchen, getting hot and bothered and have her curls uncurling. Also, they were both going to be nervous and a starter such as this did not require any special skill to eat it. There was a lamb moussaka to follow. It was already made and safely in the fridge. All that was needed was for her to pop it in the oven to heat up when John arrived and some frozen peas would be the perfect accompaniment. She had thought long and hard over pudding and in the end had settled on a spongy flan with fruit and jelly on top, only to realise with horror that it was not particularly diabetic-friendly and so changed her mind to cheese and a rather anaemic-looking fruit salad made of oranges, apples, bananas and green grapes but no added sugar.

Typically, when Joan wanted everything to run like clockwork, Ivy was late home, the driver of the bus dropping off clients having chosen today of all days to try an alternative route. Knowing that Ivy's normal routine was to sit on the sofa and fall asleep – goodness only knew what they got up to at the day centre but she inevitably returned shattered – Joan's plan was to herd her up to bed immediately. She had her own little television in there, if she wanted it, but she could be snug and cosy in bed – in other words, out of the way.

Ivy was bothered by this unexpected change and announced that she didn't want to go to bed yet, that she wasn't tired and she wanted scrambled eggs and bacon for supper.

Joan promised her a tray in her room which went some way to mollifying her mother though she repeatedly kept trying to come back down the stairs as she was pushed up them, baffled by this change in the routine she was used to.

Exasperated, Joan decided that there was only one solution. An extra sleeping tablet. A double dose of that particular medication had worked well the day that Joan had left Simeon in charge. Ivy had come to no harm, apart from the bowel incident, which was obviously something nobody would expect a small boy to take care of.

Something of a struggle ensued as, despite her protestations, Ivy was stripped to underclothes, over which a nightdress was thrown and a large clean incontinence pad stuffed into her pants. Still complaining, she was wrong footed, sat down heavily on the bed and before she realised where she was, her sheet had been tucked in securely and the duvet arranged neatly on top of her. Knowing that she would have forgotten about the request for scrambled eggs and bacon, Joan took her a mug of tea, a sausage roll and a jam tart and waited while she innocently swallowed the medication that was due without noticing that there were two extra tablets.

Joan left the tablets to exert their soporific effect and went to have a quick bath, exfoliate (she had read about this in a magazine at the hairdresser's but still wasn't quite sure what to do) and then apply a rather heavy layer of makeup, most of which she then decided to remove as she thought she looked overly vampish. She cut her leg while shaving it and the bleeding was persistent. The required plaster was effective but unattractive but with any luck she'd be able to slip to the toilet and remove it in a couple of hours' time.

On her bed, ready laid out, was her outfit for tonight. Everything was brand new. It had to be because it was all symbolising the start of a new life. Sheer, almost black, sensual hold ups, matching bra and pants went on first. She felt empowered by the audacity of her outfit. So unlike her or anything she had had before. Never, ever had she made any sort of effort for a man simply because she had never met anyone whom she felt deserved it, until now.

Her candy-pink dress had elbow-length sleeves and a high neck, but the way it clung to her body left nothing to the imagination. She hadn't been entirely sure that she had the figure to carry it off but the shop assistant had been insistent that just no one could look better in it than her, even some celebrity who had tried it on only the day before. It had cost a staggering amount of money, from an exclusive boutique she had once heard someone recommend, enough for forty of the normal sort of dresses she might look for from a well- known high street store. But this moment was worth it all. Everything, without exception had to be right and so far it was.

A crash came from Ivy's room and Joan rushed to see what it was, anxious lest her mother was on the floor again. Fortunately, she was still tucked up, now snoring heavily and must have stretched one arm out which had knocked her alarm clock off the table. Joan replaced it with care. She knew her mother was very particular about being able to see what time it was, were she to wake up. It was a shame that her mother wasn't awake to see her daughter in all her glory, looking magnificent and glorious. She was barely recognisable.

The door bell resonated around the house, causing Joan to jump and Ivy to start, mid-snore.

The moment was nigh!

With every ounce of control that she possessed, which was so hard when she was feeling like an unexploded bomb with an ever-shortening lit fuse, Joan left her bedroom, leaving the door ajar for once. How awful would it be if, while they were in the process of tearing each other's clothes off, panting with mutual lust and she had to stop and unlock the door?

With one final check in the mirror, she inhaled deeply, exhaled even more deeply and walked elegantly down the stairs to the front door.

Chapter Thirty-two

From the moment he had woken John had had a good feeling, which persisted throughout his day. Outside it was more than agreeably mild and there was nothing he was particularly dreading at work, which always helped. Yes, it was busy but fulfilling as at no point did he feel that it was out of his control and the two consultants he wanted to speak to had both been in their office when he had rung.

His patients had been an interesting mix of routine follow-ups, minor illnesses and conundrums, enough of the latter to spark his interest but not wonder how the dickens he was going to cope. He diagnosed a new case of overactive thyroid, saw a very satisfying response to steroids in a sixty-five-year-old woman whom he suspected had polymyalgia rheumatica and he received a banana from an elderly gentleman whose rash had cleared up with the cream prescribed. As always, it was the little things that meant the most and he ate it at coffee time, while Ellie was watching.

John's good mood must have been infectious because the ambience at the surgery seemed more relaxed than usual. Something he couldn't put his finger on for quite a while but the reception area was bustling along quietly and hopefully efficiently, Gary and Elizabeth were full of smiles and having some appropriate banter with the patients, Gemma looked happy manning the telephone and Elliott was even heard to be whistling at one point.

He had run more or less to time with his surgeries, which had been both fully booked and boasted a one-hundred-per-cent attendance rate, so this was hopefully a promising sign that Joan was reverting to her normal efficient self. As he thought this, it occurred to him that he hadn't seen her all day. It was most unlike her not to knock on the door and ask if she could 'just bob in for a moment or two' before he started each surgery and afterwards as well (and during if she got her way) on the pretext of checking that he had everything he needed, whether he required coffee or tea, would he like to put in an order for a sandwich for lunch and a variety of other messages and platitudes, some of which actually had a bearing on a specific patient.

Up in the common room, he came across Clare, busy tidying up some odds and ends and enjoying a Cornish pasty.

'Have you seen Joan today?' he asked her, settling down to do some of his own paperwork before leaving for the day.

'She's off sick,' Clare reported. 'Elliott said that she had a terrible headache. A migraine or something similar. She's rung to say she'll be back tomorrow.'

'Oh dear. I've been seeing her for months about headaches. They've never sounded like migraines from her description of them and I can never find any signs when I examine her. I've always assumed that they're stress related.'

'They probably are. She's an odd woman. She used to be so reliable and constant but recently she's seemed tense and, well, a little bit bonkers, if I'm honest.'

John chuckled. 'I know what you mean. Be grateful she's not in charge of your messages. She drives me crazy sometimes with all the snippets she apparently cannot possibly email but must talk to me about and pass on. Most I can't make head or tail of. Did Elliott tell you what she's been doing with my appointments?'

Clare shook her head and he gave her a quick outline.

'We're discussing it next week at our partners' meeting and she's supposed to show that she's improved before then,' John went on.

'That's outrageous!' Clare was appalled. 'Whatever induced her to do such a thing?'

'Who knows? Maybe she thought that it was a way of thanking

me for looking after her mother…talking of whom, I am supposed to visit on my way home. Thank goodness she came up in conversation otherwise I'd have completely forgotten.'

Clare paused. 'There was something I wanted to speak to you about, if you've time, John.'

'Of course, though I know what you're going to tell me. You're pregnant, aren't you?'

'How on earth did you know?' Clare laughed. 'Yes I am! Nearly twelve weeks and everything is going so much better than last time, not that it could have been worse, let's face it.' She looked at the half-eaten pasty in her hand. 'I am so hungry with this one!'

John gave her a big hug. 'I am so pleased for you and David. Congratulations! It's obviously going to be a little girl.'

'That would be so perfect. I had my first scan the day before yesterday and all's well. Ed's wife Zoe did it for me. She's so lovely and understanding. She makes me feel very safe.'

'Do you know something, Clare?' John commented, 'I've had a really good day today and this news is the icing on the cake. Have you told the others yet?'

'I wanted to tell you first. Senior partner and all that…'

'Thank you. I am honoured.' He pretended to bow.

John was genuinely delighted for Clare and David. Their first-born had been a long time coming and the pregnancy and delivery far from easy. Hopefully, they would be blessed with a far more straightforward few months second time around. Checking his watch, he rang Faye to share Clare's news and report that he was off to visit Ivy and should be home within the hour, all being well.

'I've got to bring up the subject of long-term residential care today,' he explained. 'So depending on how Joan reacts, I might be a bit longer. I'm not looking forward to trying to persuade her that we are very close to the time when this is the only viable option.'

'She's wonderful how she's coped up until now,' Faye replied.

'But the cracks are beginning to appear, thick and fast, sadly. I'd really like to avert a crisis if I can.'

'Well, darling, if anyone can, you can. If you can't, then you'll have done your best. Take care and I'll see you when I see you.'

Chapter Thirty-three

John was stamping his feet on Joan's doorstep, feeling the chill in the early evening air. He was less than enthusiastic about the visit and wanted to get it over with as quickly as possible but Joan was taking longer than usual to let him in. He noticed while he waited that there was no sign of a light in the lounge; usually he could spot some as the curtains never quite seemed to meet in the middle. Perhaps she was upstairs still in bed with a bad head. He was feeling rather guilty about her being off sick. Surely he would have spotted the diagnosis of a common condition like migraine? What if it wasn't that but something worse? Despite his repeated questioning, had he missed vital clues? His mouth was becoming dry as his imagination played tricks with him and he noticed that his palms were a little sweaty with anxiety.

Should he go? Perhaps telephone from home? It would have been wiser to do this before he set off, with hindsight, as he might have been able to save himself a trip in the first place. Should he wait a bit longer? Think of finding an open window? Call the police? Break in? Now he was really starting to worry.

Luckily he heard the unmistakable sounds of the door being unlocked before he needed to make a decision and a huge sense of relief swept over him.

'Ah, Joan,' he began but then stopped in his tracks as he caught sight of her. She certainly didn't look ill, resplendent in a dress that looked as though it had been sprayed on her, fully made up and smelling like a perfume counter in a department store.

He cleared his throat. 'Well! How glamorous you're looking! Are you off out somewhere or having friends round?'

'Just one very special friend,' Joan purred, taking his coat with some force as he had not been planning to take it off.

John wandered into the lounge where flickering candlelight cast an almost mediaeval glow around the room. She had certainly gone to a lot of trouble for someone. It wasn't to his taste though.

'Here, have a drink, please,' demanded Joan, appearing suddenly from the kitchen, where she had run to put her moussaka in the oven. She handed him a flute of champagne.

'My word! I wasn't expecting this. You're obviously pulling out all the stops for this friend. I'm really pleased for you if you've met someone.'

'Oh, I've known him for a long time but we're about to take our relationship to a new level.'

'Er, right.' How awkward was this?

Why did Joan insist on standing so close to him? Was it because it was so dark that she couldn't see him?

'Now then, where's Ivy and how's she been? I mustn't disrupt your evening.'

'Oh, she's upstairs. Asleep in all probability. She wanted an early night. Worn out by the day centre. So we can just sit and enjoy our drinks. Please...' she gesticulated towards the sofa, 'sit down. You said you wanted to talk to me and I have so much I need to say to you.'

She's presenting me with the ideal opportunity to talk about Ivy, so that's good, thought John, settling into the cushions and taking a sip of his drink.

'It's interesting that you find she's worn out by the day centre, Joan. Sadly, I think it's another sign that her dementia and general condition are getting worse. The report from there agrees with this; they too have noticed that there has been a significant deterioration. There's no easy way to say this and please do not for one moment think that this is any criticism whatsoever on your care, but I think it's time to consider long-term care for her, seriously and as soon as you can.'

'Oh absolutely,' panted Joan, feeling a bit giddy after champagne on an empty stomach.

John didn't quite pick up on this and carried on. 'You must remember that you have your own life to lead and Ivy would want you to do that.'

Joan stared at her knees, overcome by his suggestion briefly but then reading the subliminal message in his words. It would remove another obstacle that stood in the way of their ideal future.

'Do you really think that?'

'Of course I do. You've lots of life ahead of you to enjoy and do new things, have new friendships. Putting your mother into long-term care isn't giving up on her; it's what's best for her. You'll be able to visit as often as you want but at the same time know that she's safe and being well looked after. All of which will give you more time to do the things you want and spend more time with Simeon.'

'He's going to live with his father,' she announced.

'Goodness! That seems a bit sudden.' John was quite taken aback. 'How does he feel about that?'

'Oh, he's thrilled to bits. So I'll be on my own...but not for long...'

Joan stared into his eyes. This was her cue. Daringly she rested her hand lightly on his knee. This was it! Now or never...

'You're right,' she uttered in a husky, supposedly attractive voice, 'about everything. I understand what you're telling me and I'm with you all the way. I don't know how I'd manage without you. Thank you.'

He patted her hand without giving this gesture a thought. Why should he? He must have done it a million times before when comforting distressed patients. Anyway, he had been expecting all sorts of convoluted arguments why Ivy ought to stay at home, Joan insisting she was able to cope, digging her heels in, refusing to make changes, so he had got off extraordinarily lightly. Amazing! He allowed himself some more champagne. It was quite delicious and to his fairly educated palate tasted very expensive. He made a comment to this effect.

'So glad you like it. We'll have our starters in a minute. Let me top you up.'

At that moment, John was aware of a strong feeling of unease and a strong desire to get away. What was she talking about? Starters? What starters?

Joan was not only behaving most peculiarly but she also had a very odd look on her face. She recharged his glass and then sat back down, even closer to him, far too close for his comfort, her thigh rubbing against his, a deliberate action without any doubt. She had pulled her dress up to show most of her thighs. He tried to edge away from her but she shuffled after him until he was rammed up against the arm of the sofa, leaning back to avoid her approaching face and garish clown-like red lips.

'Don't be shy,' she whispered, taking his glass from him and putting it on the table. 'This is our moment.'

'Er, Joan, what do you think you're doing?'

'It's time.'

'Time? Time for what?'

'For us! We've been fighting our feelings for so long but we both know we can't go on like this any longer. We want, no we need, we must be as one.'

'What nonsense is this? Is this some sort of joke? Or are you rehearsing for a play?'

Joan drew back slightly and laughed. 'Oh, you're so amusing. How alike we are in so many ways. Our senses of humour, our outlook on life, our likes, our dislikes...'

'Are you drunk?'

'Only on love!'

She lunged at him and John found himself pinned to the back of the sofa in a most uncomfortable way, whipping his head from side to side to avoid her attempts to kiss him. With a degree of necessary force, he pushed her away and took the opportunity to leap to his feet, instantly feeling less like a trapped animal. Joan sprawled across the sofa but quickly pulled herself together. She stood up to face him and sinuously wound her arms around his neck in what she felt was a sensuous way.

'I love you,' she breathed, 'and I know you feel the same.'

'What are you talking about? Are you mad? Of course I don't love you. I'm very happily married.'

'We have been drawing closer for months. Our attraction is indestructible. We are inseparable.'

John held her away from him, his hands on her shoulders, wanting to prevent her getting any nearer to him.

'Come to your senses, woman. There's nothing between us. There's been some awful misunderstanding on your part, Joan. I haven't a clue where you got this idea from but it's pure fantasy. You've been under a lot of strain, I know. Perhaps this is a sign that it's all too much for you now.'

'But I know you love me! Look what you've done! You've come to see me away from work every week, pretending you were checking on my mother! You gave me chocolates for helping you! You gave me your home phone number and said I could ring you anytime.'

John closed his eyes briefly. 'Oh, Joan, I would do those things for any patient if it was necessary. Ivy is my patient. I'm sorry if you've read far more into this, which you clearly have. I've never, ever given you the merest hint that our relationship is any more than doctor–patient or doctor and receptionist.'

'You arranged for me to come to your house every Saturday when your wife was away!'

'That was Faye's idea. To help you earn a bit more money.'

'No! I kissed you when you were ill! You told me you loved me!'

'What? Well, you shouldn't have. I must have been delirious,' John reprimanded her abruptly, having heard enough, but Joan was a long way off finishing.

'But all those consultations. You gazing into my eyes with your light, holding my hand while you've taken my blood pressure, asking me to come back to see you again and again.'

John was incredulous. 'That's how any doctor would look after a patient with headaches...'

Joan snorted in disbelief. 'Rubbish! There was more to it than that, you know there was. You kept on asking me to come back. Don't you see what this all means? We are drawn to each other in a way that is magical!'

'Joan, Joan, Joan. Where is all this coming from? Can't you see that you've let your imagination run away with you? I don't love you. I never have and I never will.'

She looked desperate. Part of her hair had escaped from its overdose of hair spray and dangled, lacklustre, down her forehead. Her mascara was beginning to run down her cheeks as angry tears trickled from her eyes.

'But I sent you cheese and wine at Christmas and a huge Easter egg for diabetics. I admit the chocolates were a mistake but I didn't know then. And that beautiful Valentine's card. The risks I've taken to protect you at work and all the while, you knew, I know you did, that I was doing it because we were in love and just counting the days until you retired.'

'I'm sorry, Joan. None of this is true. You must realise this.'

She seemed to deflate before him as though she had a slow puncture and he let go of her shoulders, in the belief that she was going to sit down. He turned, looking to see where he had put his medical bag, planning to go up and see Ivy and then hopefully get off home. As soon as he took his eyes off her, she bounded at him, thumping him with her fists, clenched so hard that her knuckles were white, slapping him, kicking him, screaming abuse at the top of her voice, possessed by so much anger that she was on the point of exploding. Trying to fight her off was difficult. He didn't want to hurt her but this had to stop. She was hysterical and screaming.

'You love me! I know! Admit it! Go on! We're going to be married!'

At a loss because she was beyond the point of listening to what he had to say, he slapped her across the cheek and in the moment's silence that followed as she took in his action, aware of the burning sensation where his hand had landed, the ceiling shook as there was an almighty thud immediately up above them.

This was not quite how Joan had anticipated the earth moving for her that evening.

'Oh my God! Ivy!' shouted John, running out of the room and up the stairs, three at a time, arriving breathless and coughing.

The poor old woman was on the floor, one leg crumpled under her, the other sticking out at an odd angle. On her face, the look was a mix of bewilderment, total confusion and pain.

'Where am I?' she wailed.

'Ring for an ambulance! Now!' John yelled at the top of his voice. He knew he had left his mobile phone in the car and hoped that Joan might come to her senses enough to be able to manage this task.

Gently he tried to do what he could to make Ivy as comfortable as possible, given the circumstances. He stroked her frail, freckly hand, covered her up to keep her warm and pushed her wispy, white hair out of her eyes, talking to her all the while about anything he could think of, reassuring her that help was on the way and would arrive at any minute.

Joan appeared at the doorway, shaking from head to toe.

'Did you ring?' barked John.

'Yes, yes, I did. It's on its way. What's wrong with her?'

'She's fallen out of bed. I suspect she's fractured her hip and maybe hit her head as she's incredibly drowsy.'

'But I gave her extra sleeping tablets,' she confessed. 'So we wouldn't be disturbed.'

John looked up at Joan and sadly shook his head. 'How could you? The sooner she gets into care, the better,' he said, sternly.

As the befuddled Ivy was transferred to a stretcher and carried down the stairs as carefully as possible, followed by a whimpering Joan, John stood up and stretched out. His trousers were damp and smelly from Ivy's incontinence, as were his hands. Unable to do anything about the former, he wandered onto the landing and headed for the bathroom, or rather what he presumed was the bathroom as it was the only open door. He switched on the light, instantly realising that this was Joan's bedroom and was on the point of leaving when he was rooted to the ground with shock.

It was like walking into some weird fairground ride. Everywhere he looked, he saw his own face leering back at him. Every square centimetre of the wallpaper was covered with photos of himself. Hundreds of them. On the walls, the ceiling, the windowsill and every available surface as well. The ones she had taken for the newsletter, printed out dozens of times, small versions, enlargements, some monochrome, others in brassy Technicolor.

And another by the bed, no, hang on, that was one of the photos from his house! What had been a lovely one of him and Faye on holiday was now a rather eerie one of him and a totally out of proportion cut-out of Joan.

Trying to recreate his bedroom, she had bought the same bed linen as him, the same curtains. A pair of his pyjamas was folded neatly on one set of pillows adjacent to something cream and diaphanous on the others. He dreaded to think what that might be.

Standing, gazing round at this shrine dedicated to him, spellbound by what he saw, John was simultaneously aghast and revolted. Joan was completely out of her mind. He felt physically sick but at the same time was transfixed by the horror of it all. He had no idea what was the cause of all this but one thing was certain and that was that Joan needed some urgent help.

Chapter Thirty-four

John wrongly assumed that Joan would go with Ivy in the ambulance. Not so. On his arrival back in the hallway, she was waiting for him, reaching out as soon as she saw him, wanting him to take her in his arms and console her.

'Finally, it's just the two of us.'

He neatly stepped out of the way, thinking quickly.

'Joan, run up to your mum's room and pack a few things for her. You know the sort of stuff, then I'll give you a lift to the hospital.'

She shot him a pleading look. He nodded encouragingly.

'Off you go. I'm going to ring the Emergency department and have a word in advance of your mum's arrival. Quickly now, she's going to wonder where she is and where you are. It's important that she has a familiar face with her.'

Hoping that she was out of earshot, he didn't ring the hospital. He had had no intention of doing so but instead rang Faye quickly and then Clare.

'Is David there?' he gabbled.

'Hi, John! What? No, I'm sorry, he's still at the hospital; he's on call. Can I help?'

He explained. 'Oh my word! The woman is obsessed with you. Look, I'll get in touch with David immediately and he'll meet you in A&E. Does she need sectioning, do you think?'

'Possibly. If you can do that, that'd be great. See you soon. I've got to try to get her there now.'

'Good luck. Ring again if you need any help.'

He hurriedly finished his call as the sound of Joan returning was apparent.

'Darling,' she began, as though the previous discussion had never taken place. 'Now we can be alone, at last. Let me see how the moussaka is getting on – it's smelling delicious, don't you think, and I'll pour you another drink. What an eventful evening we've had! I think we deserve one, don't you? But at least there won't be any more interruptions now...'

Clearing his throat, John braced himself. 'I think we need to go to the hospital and see how your mother is.'

Joan turned down the corners of her mouth. 'We can ring in a bit. Let's talk about us and our future. I thought we should live in your house, at least to start with... Faye can move out, you can get a divorce quite quickly these days...'

'Don't start all that again.'

'You know I'm right. Don't try to fight it, darling John. Shall we go to the bedroom now?'

The pout increased in meaningfulness and it occurred to John that arguing with her was going to achieve absolutely nothing. Better to play along, though the thought was perfectly repugnant to him. He turned to her after a deep breath in.

'You know what? The night is young. Let's go for a drive in my car. Dinner's going to be a while, isn't it? We can pick up some more champagne while we're out.'

Her face transformed in an instant as though a magic eraser had been passed over it. Back were the sparkling eyes, the trembling lips, her hands trying to touch him, stroke him, worship him.

'Oh yes! Do I need a coat?'

'Yes, I think so. It's very chilly out there tonight.'

'Won't be a tick!'

She skipped up the stairs, in a girlish fashion, pausing repeatedly to look back at him and give a little wave, which he felt honour bound to return but felt ridiculously foolish doing so. Back in an instant, if she had noticed that John had been in her bedroom, she gave no sign of it. She took his arm, proprietarily, cuddling up to his side, rubbing her cheek on the rather scratchy tweed of his coat. Her eyes were closed in bliss.

Her head remained resting on his shoulder as he drove, which made changing gears somewhat hazardous but thanks to some quiet roads, they made good progress. Her continual chatter about how she loved him and how their future was to pan out occupied her for the whole of the journey and it was only when they drew into the hospital car park that she sat up and asked why they were there.

'I have to check on a patient,' John answered truthfully. 'Please come with me. There's someone I'd like you to meet as well.'

'Oh, of course. That's what doctors' wives have to do.'

The charge nurse in the Emergency Department informed them that Ivy was in radiology but everything pointed to a fractured hip. He pointed to a room where they could wait.

'You're waiting for Dr Jennings as well aren't you?' he inquired, glancing at Joan. 'I'll give him a call.'

John nodded. Joan's ears pricked up.

'Dr Jennings? What's she doing here? Is she ill?'

Leading her into the consultation room, John sat her down but she refused to let go of his arm.

'Clare is fine. I've asked her husband to come and have a chat with you. Is that okay?'

'Why?'

'You're not yourself. You need some help and he's the best person to do that.'

Joan looked affronted. 'I don't need any help.'

'I'm worried about you,' John said softly. 'I care what happens to you.'

She spun round. 'You're worried about me? You care? I can't remember the last time anyone worried about me. Simeon doesn't care about me one bit. He's rude, has no manners and no respect. My mother would love me if she recognised who I was.

'Do you know what it's like to feel alone in the world? Having to give everything you have to others and receive nothing back? It's no reason to live. But then I saw you in a different light, fell in love with you and knew you loved me. You just haven't grasped this yet. You soon will.'

'So you'll talk to him?'

'I'm not sure.'

'For me? Talk to him for me?'

'I'll do anything for you.'

Chapter Thirty-five

'De Clerambault's syndrome or erotomania.'

David had no doubt about the diagnosis after spending an hour or more with Joan. Paranoid delusions of the amorous sort, usually in a woman, who believes that an older person of higher social status is in love with them.

'What?' asked John and Faye, simultaneously, totally baffled.

David laughed. 'It's not common. She's agreed to stay in for a couple of days so that I can assess her fully.'

It was the following day, when he and Faye had popped round to the house to find out more. They were in the lounge, a comfortable room with homely furniture and most of the carpet hidden by a plethora of toys.

Clare was making coffee and listening, while Tom, their young son, was captivated by a wooden train track laid out on the carpet, complete with cantilever bridge, station and two tunnels. Faye was on her knees, neatly negotiating an engine and four carriages full of zoo animals round a series of bends.

'I'm sure that's the right thing, don't you, John?' offered Clare, bringing in a tray of mugs and a plate of biscuits, some chocolate, some plain. She placed the plate with the latter facing John, who reached over and took one of the former. Faye pretended not to notice.

'Without a doubt. Regardless of how she's been with me, she's been behaving completely out of character at work, though I suppose it could all be part of the same thing, could it, David?'

'Maybe. Change of personality is an important sign though. I've ordered a CAT scan for her. That'll probably be today or tomorrow, all being well.'

'You should have seen her bedroom. I was speechless. Most people would have nightmares with all those photos of me staring at them.'

He helped himself to another chocolate biscuit. Faye affected a stage cough, which he ignored. It was a very special occasion. Not the usual sort however which is associated with celebration and joy. No, this one was the total opposite. Though he was laughing with them, he was shocked and unnerved by what had happened. He kept thinking back, wondering if he had encouraged her in some way or other. Faye, David and Clare had all assured him that he had not, that he had simply been his normal friendly self, treating her no differently to any of the other staff. Despite their consoling words, guilt still haunted him. Should he have spotted this developing? Had he missed all the clues?

In all honesty, he had heard of the syndrome but only remembered it because it was one of those interesting facts that nestle down in the mind, only to be rarely, if ever used; he had certainly never encountered it in practice before.

He felt sad for Joan, imagining her on the ward, wondering what was going on, presumably still thinking about him and probably looking at photos of him on her mobile phone – if she was allowed access to it. He felt sorry for Ivy too, having her hip operated on, her dementia getting worse and worse but at least a bed would be found for her in a nursing home, if she managed to avoid a post-operative pneumonia, where she would be well looked after and, hopefully, happy in her own world. Then there was the boy, Simeon. All his life ahead of him. What a relief that his father had come on the scene to provide some stability. He needed it so badly after a worryingly confusing start.

As her obsession with John had taken over, Joan seemed to have forgotten all about her family. She had told David how impossible she found Simeon and his ways, how, against all her better judgements, she had rung Greg and pleaded with him to become involved with his son, so that she could have some well-earned respite. And while John was the innocent party, he managed to feel guilty and sad about this too.

All those missed opportunities to encourage her to talk, tell him how she was really feeling, the truth about what was going on in her life at home, the troubles associated with being a constant carer for someone, her fears, her lack of support. As he berated himself, he forgot how he had indeed repeatedly asked her if she had worries, how he had always suspected that she did have and how he tried his hardest to get her to open up to him. But she had chosen not to. The chances had been there, it was her prerogative to remain silent if she wanted.

Without thinking, he reached for a third chocolate biscuit, after which Clare tactfully removed the plate and put it on the sideboard.

He was still fretting when they got home. Faye had suggested they stop off at a pub that did very decent Italian food but even this failed to revive his spirits and all he did was push a helping of lasagne around his plate and drink three glasses of red wine, large ones, in quick succession.

As they entered the house, his mobile phone rang. It was David. 'Hi, John, I thought you'd like to know. Sadly, Joan's CAT scan shows that she has a large tumour in her left frontal lobe. That accounts for the change in personality for sure. It just so happened that in her case it developed into De Clerambault's syndrome.'

Chapter Thirty-six

Faye found her husband standing in the kitchen, ashen, mobile phone in hand, mouth slightly agape. He was trembling from head to toe.

'Whatever is it, darling?' she asked, panic stricken, pulling out a chair and helping him into it before he fell over. 'Are you ill?'

As if suddenly aware that she was beside him, he looked at her strangely.

'It's Joan. She has a brain tumour...in her frontal lobe. That's why she changed. Her mind changed, her personality.'

'Oh my goodness. That poor woman. As if she hasn't had enough to cope with. Life can be so cruel at times. Can they operate?'

Shrugging his shoulders, 'I don't know. She's to see a neurologist and maybe a neurosurgeon,' he replied.

'I'm sure that's the last thing you were expecting. Thankfully, it's been found and hopefully they can do something to help her.'

He pulled himself upright and stumbled into the lounge whereupon he poured the largest brandy Faye had ever seen him drink. She sat next to him on the sofa but he had flashbacks of Joan heaving her body towards him and so he moved to an armchair, where he sat, leaning forwards, head in hands.

To her horror, Faye saw that he was crying, something she had never seen before. He was always so strong and able to cope. Far from being emotionless, he was one of life's stalwarts, ever dependable and to be relied on in any crisis.

'John! Whatever's wrong?'

It was moments before he replied. 'It's all my fault.'

'What is?' She put her arms around him, feeling her heart ache for him as he sobbed on her shoulder.

'Joan.'

'What makes you say that? You've been a fabulous GP to her, just as you are with all your patients.'

'I've made a huge mistake.'

'John, you mustn't beat yourself up like this. I'm sure you haven't. Remember what David said, when we were there. That syndrome is incredibly rare. None of the others at work had a clue about the diagnosis. Agreed, they all thought she was behaving oddly but there must be a million and one reasons for doing that.'

'I can accept that but there's more to it than that.'

'In what way?'

'Her headaches. She'd been coming to see me for months with headaches that I could never get to the bottom of. They must have been a sign of the tumour. I was going to refer her to a specialist but she refused, more than once. If only I'd insisted, then maybe we'd have picked it up earlier and more could be done.'

Faye thought for a moment. 'John, I don't think you can see this clearly at the moment. You've got to get this into perspective. You know as well as I do that if a patient comes in to you with headaches then you take it very seriously, you always take a good history and do whatever examination is necessary. One of the reasons that you are such a well-respected GP is that you know your patients as people and that you relish that part of your job. You pick up on all the clues too, such as what they're wearing, how they hold themselves, are they happy or sad, nervous or probably hiding something. You will have done exactly the same with Joan. If anything, because she's a member of staff, you'll have given a little bit extra and before you start making mountains out of molehills about that comment, all I meant was that you'll have seen her as an extra patient at the end or beginning of surgery, so as not to disrupt her day.'

'I did, you're right. How boringly predictable I am. I cannot comprehend, though, why I didn't pick up on this. It all seems so obvious to me now.'

Faye hugged him tight. 'Of course it does now. It always does with hindsight. At the time, you did what was right at that moment, with the information you had at your fingertips. Nobody could have done more. Some would have done considerably less. Please, believe me.'

No matter how reassuring she tried to be, no matter how many times she repeated that he was not at fault, no matter how many times she hugged him tight and said nothing, he continued to tremble. No medicinal benefit was obtained from the brandy. It didn't even make him feel drunk, only sicker and more anxious. Bed was not an option, no matter how much Faye tried to coax him to go upstairs with her. Sleep was going to be impossible while his thoughts circulated round and round, over and over, like a mixed-up roller coaster, each circuit making him feel increasingly responsible for Joan's illness. Whichever way he looked at it, the finger pointed at him.

Eventually, Faye capitulated, sprinted up to get their duvet and then persuaded John to return to the sofa so that they were close together. She held him in his arms for the entire night, waiting until he had nodded off before snatching a few moments shallow sleep, all the while on guard lest he needed her. They awoke, stiff and sore, Faye with pins and needles in her hand, her arm having got trapped behind John's head.

'Stay at home today, John,' she suggested as they sipped piping hot tea and snuggled under the duvet. 'You're in no fit state to work.'

He was insistent. 'I have to go. I have to get answers to questions and find out if I'm responsible. I'm not going to be able to relax until I have. Don't worry, I'll be fine. How much sleep I've had is irrelevant. Like the old days when we did our own on call. I need to shower first and get some clean clothes.'

Quite how he managed to see eighteen patients in morning surgery will forever be one of those unanswered questions. But he did, competently, a consummate professional to the last, concentrating so intently on what was in front of him that for a couple of hours, he was able to push his worries and fears to the back of his mind.

As Mrs Somersby waddled out of the room after her antenatal check – she was due in two days – John's heart sank as thoughts of Joan came flooding back. He needed to talk to someone about her but couldn't decide who. David, of course, was the obvious choice but maybe the consultant neurologist was a better bet to start with.

Dry mouthed, heart pumping furiously, he dialled the number of the hospital. He was informed by the ward that Joan was very settled and had been seen by Dr Sinclair first thing that morning. He asked to be transferred to Dr Sinclair's office and was greeted by a grumpy secretary whose manner changed to one of charm and friendliness when she realised that this was not yet another patient on the phone trying to bargain for an earlier appointment.

'He's out on the wards,' she explained. 'But I'll get him to ring you. I can't say when it'll be. Hopefully today.'

'Thanks.'

His only option was to wait. Dr Sinclair had to do his job as well as return calls from agitated general practitioners. It might be any time. He would simply have to carry on with his day and hope his call was returned. If not, another sleepless night lay ahead.

Sighing, he checked some blood results, left messages for patients and electronically signed off three dozen repeat prescriptions. There were four booked telephone calls with patients, two of whom were ringing him, so when his phone rang John was fully expecting to talk to either Jane Inkerman about her contraceptive pill or Harry Mason-Phillips about 'a personal matter, patient prefers not to say'.

'Good morning,' boomed a voice. 'Vincent Sinclair here.'

John was quite sure that his heart had stopped altogether. He gulped. 'Good morning. John Britton. I'm grateful to you for ringing back so quickly.'

'Had a couple of free moments. How can I help?'

'I think you've seen one of my patients this morning, Joan Bickerdike. She was admitted under the psychs with de Clerambault's syndrome.'

'Ah yes, absolutely fascinating. She's certainly developed quite a crush on you!'

John tried to join in with the roar of laughter that was so loud, he had to move the receiver from his ear.

'The thing is, I'd been seeing her for months, with headaches and now I've found out that she has a tumour, I'm so concerned that I've missed something. Please, be honest with me. Have I?'

'My dear John, relax.'

John could visualise Dr Sinclair sitting at his desk in a pin-striped suit.

'To start off with, probably only about half the people with brain tumours will present with headache. Next, on careful examination, she has no physical signs. Her only presenting feature is the personality change. Finally and most importantly in this case – and I was going to ring you anyway to discuss this – is that when I saw her today, she told me categorically that she has had headaches most of her life and they haven't changed in any way, shape or form. Yes, she did initially go to see you with headaches, but that was because it gave her an excuse to see you, to have you close to her when you examined her eyes. And because you're a good GP and followed her up carefully, you played right into her hands.

'In all honesty, you could not have done anything more. We're sending her across to Leeds to see the neurosurgeons tomorrow. They've seen her scans and they'll probably operate.

'So calm yourself. By the sounds of it, you've had a pretty rough time with this one.'

'Will she be ok?'

'A tad early to tell. There are some suspicious signs on the CAT scan, suggesting that it might be a malignant tumour, so we'll need to know the histology before we can start talking about prognoses.'

'How dreadful. Look, I cannot begin to tell you how grateful I am for your time and how relieved I am.'

'Any time, John. Must dash now. Ring me any time if you want to chat more.'

'Thanks, I owe you one.'

Maybe Joan had had headaches all her life and now John's head was on the point of bursting, or so it felt. He rushed over to the window, opening it wide and took deep gulps of the fresh air, which both cooled and calmed him. Suddenly he was overwhelmed with fatigue. No sleep, no food, the shock of the diagnosis, the fear of having let a patient down and the self recriminations all combined into a lethal cocktail of despair and exhaustion.

His first action was to ring Faye. He needed to hear her voice and her unerring faith that she had in him. She was of course delighted, resisted the temptation to say 'I told you so' and suggested he came home for lunch and if there was time, forty winks, because if he felt anything like she did, then he was badly in need of it. He promised to, if there was time.

Upstairs in the common room, Joan was the sole topic of conversation. Clare had filled in all the details for them, having had a running report from David. Ed was googling De Clerambault's. As John entered, he was immediately included in the discussions, but no one was accusatory, just intrigued and absorbed by events. They were unanimous in that none of them would have suspected anything either.

'We're all so busy, all day,' commented Ellie. 'Perhaps her family might have noticed a change but then poor Ivy was developing dementia and that child, what's his name?'

'Simeon,' filled in John.

'That's it, Simeon. Poor kid. Well he must be so blooming mixed up about his life, how was he going to notice when something changed, let alone say anything? And if he had, the family dynamics are so fraught, who would've been able to make any sense of them and let's be honest, none of us would have thought of a brain tumour, would we?'

'I still feel guilty that I didn't pick up on the personality change,' mused John.

'Well, don't!' they said, in unison.

Chapter Thirty-seven

The Teviotdale Medical centre opened especially on the Saturday so that patients could come and wish Dr John Britton the happiest of retirements. Ellie and Clare spent the Friday evening putting up a ridiculous number of balloons round the front entrance and bunting all around the reception and main waiting areas and were back first thing in the morning to set up a huge table, which was for refreshments, provided, as a gift, by the eponymous delicatessen, Delicious.

John, who was of the opinion that this was all a little unnecessary, secretly worried how awful it would be if hardly anyone turned up and drove to the surgery, with Faye beside him, rather slowly, hoping they might encounter a traffic jam or a herd of escaped cows – anything to delay them.

His last patient he had hoped would have been more memorable than a request for a nasal spray and some cream for hard, dry skin but he had more than enough memories to take with him, the vast majority good and only a very few which were not so good. The search for a replacement partner was ongoing but at least now they had a few promising-looking candidates, on paper at least, who wanted to come and have a look round. They had sensibly decided to wait for the right person and had hired a locum to fill in until they did.

The sun was shining and it was warm enough to leave coats behind. Faye looked relaxed and happy in jeans, boat-necked striped sweater and flipflops, while John had dressed as he always did for work, cord trousers, checked shirt and his favourite jacket with the leather elbow patches. After a mildly heated discussion, he had taken Faye's advice and left his bow tie at home. It was Saturday after all.

Any worries that he might have had were needless. As they steered the car into the parking area, there was already a queue of excited people waiting at the front door. For reasons that he was unable to fathom, some were waving Union Jacks, others were cheering.

'Goodness gracious,' he spluttered to Faye.

She laughed. 'Enjoy it. This is your moment! See how people love you. But none as much as me.' She kissed him on the cheek and got out of the car, took his arm and led him to the building.

Ellie greeted them both with hugs. 'Welcome! Bucks' Fizz?' She pressed two glasses into their hands. 'Cheers! Here's to a very happy, long and healthy retirement.'

'Thank you! I can't believe all this. It's amazing.'

Over the course of the morning, there was a continual flow of patients coming in and wanting to say good-bye and thank you. A spare table had to be found, on which to put all the gifts – some wrapped to be opened later, cut flowers, plants, bottles of wine, whisky and a magnum of champagne, books, socks (why?), two paintings and an embroidered facsimile of the surgery building with all the doctors standing outside. The latter had been created by Miss Chisholm. It must have taken her hours. John noticed that he looked a bit asymmetrical and only had one leg, but it was of course the thought that mattered.

As the patients finally began to peter out, the partners, Elliott and all the practice staff gathered around, and almost had John in tears several times, with both laughter and sadness as they recounted tales from his time at the surgery. Each of them made a speech, followed by a toast and then it was John's turn.

He had prepared a rather boring and stilted speech, which he wasn't happy about and as he was about to start, he realised that it was completely inappropriate among friends such as these, so he simply said what he truly thought and as Faye said afterwards – and she had been privy to his original speech – it was straight from the heart and thus an infinite improvement.

Elliott allowed time for a round of loud applause before stepping forward.

'John, we asked you a while ago what you would like as a leaving present. Typically, your initial reaction was nothing and then with some arm twisting, you thought some posh garden furniture might be nice but to let Faye choose it. So we approached Faye and she agreed to choose your present. We hope very much that you like it and that it brings you many, many hours of happiness, fun, some exasperation possibly but much joy.'

John was puzzled. What a peculiar way to describe garden furniture. You just sat on it when it was sunny, didn't you?

But then he saw Faye's face, smiling from ear to ear and followed her gaze to where Ellie and her husband Ian had come to the fore, each one of them carrying a wriggling puppy, one black and one yellow Labrador.

'Happy retirement, John!' cried everyone.

John offered to stay and tidy up, suddenly feeling a certain reluctance to leave the surgery for the very last time. He was pushed away by Clare, who refused point blank to let him and so he moved to a corner where he sat with David, watching Tom investigate the box of toys.

'How is she?' John asked.

'She had surgery yesterday, after much prevarication,' David replied, knowing instantly who he was talking about. 'They say it went well but a lot depends on the results.'

'I still feel guilty. I know I shouldn't and I've heard what everyone's told me but that's just me, I guess, and I'll never change.'

'I expect part of you always will. That's being a doctor. You always want to get it right because you inherently care so much about your patients and doing the best you can for them. We're only human though, none of us are right all the time and that can hurt. Keep telling yourself you did nothing wrong, because that's the truth. Concentrate on all the good you've done, remember all these people who've been to see you today because they have nothing but the greatest respect for you and how you've looked after them throughout the highs and lows of their lives.'

John thought for a moment. 'That's more good advice, David. Thanks.'

'Anytime, mate. Don't forget – dinner at ours next Saturday. But now it looks as though someone needs some help…'

Faye was approaching them, juggling a puppy under each arm, with difficulty.

'Help! They've both weed on the carpet and Elliott is making tactful noises that perhaps we should take them home!'

John took the black one, which immediately began to lick his face enthusiastically. With one last look around, he stood up and took a deep breath.

'Let's go! Good job I don't have to come to work as we're going to have our hands full with these two!'